PRAISE FOR WOLF HAAS AND

BRENNER AND GOD

"Simon Brenner, the hero of Wolf Haas' marvelous series of crime thrillers, is a wildly likable and original character—a delightful and unexpected hero to show up in this noble and enduring genre. That Brenner struggles his way—always humanistically, often humorously—through Haas' acutely suspenseful narratives without the aid of a firearm, armed only with his smarts and sometimes fallible intuition, is a monumental plus." **—JONATHAN DEMME, OSCAR-WINNING DIRECTOR OF *THE SILENCE OF THE LAMBS***

"*Brenner and God* is one of the cleverest—and most thoroughly enjoyable—mysteries that I've read in a long time. Wolf Haas is the real deal, and his arrival on the American book scene is long overdue."

—CARL HIAASEN, AUTHOR OF *SICK PUPPY*

"A must for crime fiction lovers with a sense of humor: In Simon Brenner, Wolf Haas has created a protagonist so real and believable that I sometimes wanted to tap him on the shoulder and point him in the right direction!" **—ANDREY KURKOV, AUTHOR OF *DEATH AND THE PENGUIN***

"Drolly told by an unidentified yet surprisingly reliable narrator, *Brenner and God* is very funny, leavened throughout with a finely honed sense of the absurd." **—LISA BRACKMANN, *NEW YORK TIMES* BESTSELLING AUTHOR OF *ROCK PAPER TIGER* AND *GETAWAY***

"This quirkily funny kidnapping caper marks the first appearance in English of underdog sleuth Simon Brenner.... Austrian author Haas brings a wry sense of humor ... American readers will look forward to seeing more of Herr Simon." **—*PUBLISHERS WEEKLY***

"One of Germany's most loved thriller writers: he's celebrated by the literary critics and venerated by the readers."

—JOACHIM KRONSBEIN, *DER SPIEGEL*

"This is great art, great fun." **—JULIA SCHRÖDER, *GERMANY RADIO***

"The Simon Brenner books are among the funniest and best German speaking crime stories of recent years." **—*FOCUS***

"Wolf Haas writes the funniest and cleverest mysteries."**—*DIE WELT***

"With his cunning and eloquent vernacular, Wolf Haas is the most important Austrian writer working today." **—*DER STANDARD***

"He is highly entertaining... It's as if he sits on Mount Everest looking down at other thriller writers." **—*FRANKFURTER RUNDSCHAU***

BRENNER AND GOD

WOLF HAAS

BRENNER AND GOD

TRANSLATED BY ANNIE JANUSCH

BRENNER AND GOD

Originally published in German as *Brenner und der liebe Gott* by Wolf Haas

The translation of this book was supported by the Austrian Federal Ministry of Education, Arts and Culture

First Melville House printing: May 2012

Melville House Publishing
145 Plymouth Street
Brooklyn, NY 11201

www.mhpbooks.com

ISBN: 978-1-61219-113-3

Printed in the United States of America
1 2 3 4 5 6 7 8 9 10

Library of Congress Control Number: 2012936538

CHAPTER 1

My grandmother always used to say to me, *when you die, they're gonna give that mouth of yours its own funeral.* So you see, a person can change. Because today I am the epitome of silence. And it'd take something out of the ordinary to get me started. The days when everything used to set me off are over. Listen, why should every bloodbath wind up in my pint of beer? Like I've been saying for some time now, it's up to the boys to take care of. My motto, as it were.

Personally, I prefer to look on the positive side of life these days. Not just Murder He Wrote all the time, and who-got-who with a bullet, a knife, an extension cord, or what all else I don't know. Me, I'm far more interested in the nice people now, the quiet ones, the normals, the ones who you'd say—they lead their regular lives, abide by the law, don't mistake themselves for the good lord when they get up in the morning, just nice tidy lives. Propriety and all.

Look at Kressdorf's chauffeur, for example. Kressdorf, Lion of Construction, surely you know his trucks with the green letters KREBA, short for *Kressdorf Bau.* They've done a lot of work in Munich, you may have seen it, here, here, and there. And then there's this MegaLand we're getting now. But this isn't about Kressdorf, it's about his chauffeur.

Because naturally a man like Kressdorf has got a chauffeur; he can't drive himself everywhere, not a chance. Certainly not since he got married—the young bride in Vienna, the KREBA headquarters in Munich, and now a two-year-old child—simplest for them all to meet in the middle, say, in Kitzbühel. Because in Kitzbühel, of course, you've got the businesses, the contacts, you get the idea. For a child this can't be good either, back and forth all the time, and I reckon Kressdorf's daughter already thinks the autobahn is her nursery. But I have to admit she's a nice kid. Not like kids today usually are—no please, no thank you, no hello, no good-bye. Then again, it's a good thing they do behave like that, because at least that way you can tell them apart from the adults. It used to be more by size that you could tell—a small one was a child and a big one was an adult. But today the kids grow so fast that you can't use size as a point of reference anymore—is that the chief physician striding out of the maternity ward, or is it the newborn itself? And even then it's the exact opposite of how it used to be—rule of thumb, the less arrogant one's the physician.

So I was just saying, the maternity ward. Kressdorf's wife was a doctor who had her own practice, a small clinic in an office suite right downtown. A good doctor, but unfortunately a lot of problems lately with the churchgoers in front of the building, by which I mean demonstrators. They were against abortion because that was just their conviction, it shouldn't exist, a thousand reasons, the good lord, the virgin Mary and, and, *and*.

It's lucky the driver was such a robust man, because there were some days when a lankier driver would've been a lost cause. He had to smuggle the doctor's baby past those rosary-slinging rowdies like a stadium security guard who narrowly saves the referee from the lynch mob.

Now, the father's under a great deal of stress because with contractors there's always stress, and so of course the kid's got stress, too. Because today when you have two parents who don't have any time, but who do have three hundred miles of autobahn between them, then as their child, you can never escape the autobahn completely. And so you can't be angry with the child if she appoints her driver as her guardian. Believe it or not, the Kressdorf kid's first word—not "Mama," not "Papa"—"Driver." But that was at least six months ago because, in the meantime, little Helena has already started chattering so much from her car seat that the driver barely has use for the radio anymore. And above all she's good at understanding. Herr Simon's had the feeling that this child understands him better than most adults he's had anything to do with in his life. He can tell Helena the most difficult things, problems, all of it, and that two-year-old girl in the backseat understands. In return, she gives him a full report, every detail down to the hair, when he picks her up from her nanny, and Herr Simon, always the attentive listener. There was simply a kindred connection between them. Like-minded souls: understatement.

Overall, Herr Simon was quite content with his new life, which is a way of saying, he hadn't always been a chauffeur. He'd tried out different professions—more than fifty, in fact—before he found his thing. Whereas others his age were already thinking about retirement and pensions, Herr Simon was only just beginning a regular professional life.

First, the five hours from Vienna to Munich, then back five hours from Munich to Vienna, sometimes with the mother in tow, rarely with the father, but always with the amiable kid who understood him so well. Unless you were born to be a chauffeur, you can hardly imagine how much it suited him. And one thing you can't forget: Kressdorf didn't pay badly. Plagued by a guilty conscience over his child, he compensated the chauffeur exceedingly well. Or maybe it wasn't so much a guilty conscience as it was basic concern for the kid. There was never a riotous crowd in front of the abortion clinic, but somehow that silent threat from the church-types was even more menacing, because there's nothing worse than a sighing aggressor. A well-known fact: behind every mass murderer there's a mass sigher.

The Frau Doctor was thrilled about her dependable driver. That he took his job seriously goes without saying. If there was even the slightest noise somewhere, a squeal from the air-conditioning, or a faint streak left by the windshield wiper, or if a floor mat wasn't placed just so—it would have been unthinkable for him to subject the child to such a thing. Sure, he could've just said, Helena can't see the floor mat from her car seat anyway, but no, as a matter of principle, everything was always *picobello*, meticulous.

So, the chauffeur gets annoyed at himself for having forgotten to gas up yesterday just because it's never happened to him before. Five minutes into the drive out of Vienna, he glances at the gas gauge, and believe it or not, he didn't gas up last night, i.e., nothing but vapors to coast on for 190 kilometers!

Then again, maybe this was on account of the pills.

Because not all the effects were positive. A certain absent-mindedness. *It's possible the pills caused this*, the chauffeur thought, while keeping an eye out for the next gas station. He actually gave a great deal of thought to the effects of the pills. On the one hand, he wasn't sleeping so well anymore, but on the other, he was doing better since they'd been prescribed to him—where you find yourself saying, *the sun is shining a little brighter for me today*. You should know, there wasn't much wrong with him before, especially since he'd left his last girlfriend. Although in the woman's defense I should add—and, frankly, I think she left him—that she'd been at her wits' end with him. And it was his girlfriend who'd managed to get him to even go to the doctor, because all his life Herr Simon had been a crank about doctors.

But then he didn't take the pills, naysaying not only doctors but drugs, too. And just when his girlfriend had left for good, and one day the refrigerator was completely empty, the kitchen cabinets bare, canned goods and so on, pasta, rice, every last bit, so only the pills were left—only then did he take the pills. And since then—like a new man! More positive! You might have noticed it earlier today, for example, when once again the pro-life soldiers of prayer had formed a standing guard in front of the clinic. And he'd barely been able to get past them with little Helena because they were pushing from the right and the left, rosaries and embryo photos shoved right under his nose like in holy Sicily. Now, before, this would've guaranteed his hand flying out, and those plastic embryos and rosary beads would've gone scattering. But because of the pills, much calmer. And with composure you get a lot farther.

He was already twisting things around in his head at the gas station, telling himself that a minor mistake like this can happen to anyone once. And anyway, for a two-year-old even the goings-on at a gas station are interesting. She can look out the window, there are people to watch, hoses, nozzles, disposable gloves, everything. Plus, one thing you can't forget—those tizzying numbers, nothing's more beautiful to a child's soul.

So he slips out of the car as quickly as possible and closes the door behind him—you would've thought he was about to hold up the gas station—because he wants to prevent any fumes from wafting in to Helena. Because those noxious fumes, well, a little's a lot for a child. Well, I don't want to say absolutely harmful, but good, certainly not. *On second thought*, the driver says to himself—and here maybe the pills were already at work a little—*maybe a healthy child should be able to withstand a few fumes.*

While he gassed up, he made faces at Helena through the window. But to no effect; she just stared placidly back at him. And the chauffeur thought, *you see, Helena knows that at heart I'm not one to mug around*, so he assumed a normal expression, and get a load of this: then Helena smiled. You see what kind of understanding the two of them have? No wonder, when they spend so many hours together on the autobahn. Then came the window washing, though. You wouldn't believe what kind of *Hello!* that was for Helena. The chauffeur actually got nervous that the alarm would go off, what with the child giggling and pedaling her legs in the car seat as the sponge ran over the windshield, and when he squeegeed the water off, she liked that even better. So the chauffeur declared to himself, *I will always gas up on the way if she likes it so much*, and he even gave the clean passenger-side windows an extra wash, and the rear window, too, although by that point Helena wasn't getting so much out of it anymore since she couldn't turn around in her car seat.

Before he went into the shop to pay, he moved the car a few feet over to the side to where the air-pressure pump was and away from the fumes.

"I'll bring you a chocolate bar," he said as he got out of the car, because it was never *baby wanna bonbon?* or any of that other baby talk. Rather, the driver always insisted on correct German with Helena, out of principle. Chocolate wasn't entirely correct though, because the Frau Doctor had in fact impressed upon him, "No chocolate, Herr Simon. Absolutely no sugar!"

Herr Simon had explained to her a thousand times that they were just baby teeth, only there for the time being, a second pair would grow in anyway, well, not a pair, but a second crew, as it were, and when that happened, then you could always say, less chocolate. Or just don't bite all the way into it. The Frau Doctor always knew better, of course, even though it wasn't like she was a dentist, and in a private moment, the chauffeur sometimes thought to himself, *with those abortions of hers, just think how many teeth will never even find accommodations*. But arguments are useless, since she even went on to claim that chocolate was bad for the rash on Helena's hands. Otherwise, a downright nice woman. Nice, intelligent, perky figure, the works. The chauffeur even envied Kressdorf a little, but it was no mean-spirited envy, no I'd almost like to call it a positive envy, and that, too, must've been attributable to the pills. Because he said to himself, *why would a woman like the Frau Doctor seek someone like me when she can have someone like Kressdorf?* Maybe he would have thought that before, too. But before, that same thought would have railed against the wife first, the husband second, himself third, and fourth, the world at large. And today we're very much on the side of forgiveness, meaning, *Kressdorf: not such a bad guy*. Maybe the pills even exaggerated this positive perspective a bit, but one thing I should add: Kressdorf was always courteous with his chauffeur, never a crass word, never addressing him informally as *du*, but always respectfully as *Sie* and Herr Simon.

Otherwise, the KREBA chief had enemies, of course, more than enough. I don't want to sugarcoat anything now just because. But if it's about enemies, then it's his wife who's got him beat by a long shot. Because, a routine question, *do you have enemies?* As an abortion doctor you simply have a lot of people against you, it doesn't work any other way. Which is why the two of them were so happy that their daughter was in such good hands with their new chauffeur. Otherwise, they could have just hired a regular driver. But with him being a former police officer, they simply felt safer.

That they'd been so angry with him about a bar of chocolate of all things can be explained only in psychological terms. All told, his blunder with the chocolate never even would've been exposed if it hadn't been so plainly visible on the surveillance video. And when, as a parent, you look at something a hundred times, you play it a hundred times forward and backward, a hundred times over, you stop being able to see anything—except for a driver who can't make up his mind between the different kinds of chocolate bars at a gas station. And then, all of a sudden, you see the chocolate as being the culprit.

CHAPTER 2

It was an especially strange morning because something happened at the clinic, too. It began when the first patient on the morning's scheduled surgeries turned out to be an old acquaintance. You're going to say a male patient in an abortion clinic is a rare thing, but that's not the case, because family planning's a complete package, and vasectomies are performed there, too. Perfectly routine at a clinic like this.

As a matter of principle, Frau Doctor Kressdorf had great sympathy for the men who came in for vasectomies. Because men tend to leave everything else up to women, the vasectomy candidates were practically minor saints to her. However, the way she saw it, as a woman and as the director of the clinic, she was content to let the urologist perform the procedure. An exception was today's candidate, who happened to have a thing for her. You should know, Detective Peinhaupt used to know the Frau Doctor a little, back when he was starting out as a patrol officer and would always get assigned to the anti-abortionists making a racket out in front of the clinic. Since he joined the Criminal Investigation Bureau, or CRIB for short, the smaller scuffles didn't concern him anymore, and since the clinic started hiring its own private security guards, it had gotten a little quieter on the street anyway. The demonstrators had limited themselves to praying their rosaries and weren't accosting the patients anymore. You've got to picture this for yourself: to the right of the entrance is a rosary-praying anti-abortionist standing with a picture of an embryo, and to the left of the entrance—and every bit as imposing—is a bull-necked female security guard with her hair buzzed like a mowed lawn. And there between those two holy columns, the patients would get shooed through. Back when Peinhaupt was on patrol, Sykora once said to him, "pro-life versus pro-dyke," because Sykora was always joking, and Peinhaupt had made a special note of this one, but when he tried telling it to Alpha II as if he'd just come up with it himself, he didn't even crack a smile. But, okay, Alpha II was the kind of guy who couldn't be coaxed out of his shell that easily. Maybe he would've loosened up more if on his last vacation he hadn't been struck by that lightning.

It proved to be just a temporary lull for the police, because the ruckus on the street only managed to move inside the building. Believe it or not, the pro-lifers bought up, one by one, the offices surrounding the clinic. Main question: where did they get so much money from? And since the pro-lifers were the majority of the building's tenants and tried every means of getting the clinic to terminate its lease, they racked up so many power outages that the police were right back in there for the long haul.

In theory, there wasn't much the police could do about the building's tenants, and Peinhaupt even joked to the Frau Doctor once that up against a guy like Knoll, only a hitman could help. See, Knoll was the head of the pro-lifers. And it was Knoll, too, who'd scraped together the money for the property. He certainly didn't earn it selling alarm systems at Sectec. He had the best connections, no question. Obviously the Frau Doctor hadn't hired a hitman, but she did go to the newspapers when Knoll mounted surveillance cameras in the building's lobby in order to intimidate her patients. And maybe there was a moment when she did regret not hiring a hitman, because the article broke on the same day that Knoll served her with legal papers and in the same week that a water pipe broke. Peinhaupt got put on it because the matter required the police, of course. And so it was, on this of all assignments, that the brochure fell into Peinhaupt's hands. Like an advertisement that they didn't just practice abortion but prevention, too—in other words, sterilization. So he said to his colleagues on the force, *I'd never have that done.* Emasculation and all. But among men, of course, the conversation immediately got steered in the direction of *when in Rome, well then what an attractive doctor*.

In truth, Peinhaupt had entirely different reasons for a vasectomy—four, in fact, very good and very expensive reasons. Because one thing you can't forget: as a young investigator with only a few years of service behind him, he was just scraping by, netting two thousand euros, and then the bonus pay on top of it, i.e., danger, weekends, nights. And an unplanned child would have him paying roughly 340 euros. That had Peinhaupt calculating everything all over again while he was lying there on the operating table, waiting for the procedure. Because you're going to have some doubts in a situation like this. Now, he didn't jump up and run, but he did calculate the approximate price of his four children. Because it varies, depending on the age.

First for little Sandra he paid 320 euros, to the hairstylist in the Salzgries district who always said she had an IUD when the detective came by on his beat, and then one day that IUD was called Sandra. And for Benjamin it was also 320, but only for one more year, because he was already in kindergarten, and even though his mother was a kindergarten teacher, lowering the alimony didn't figure into the calculation, so it was the full 320 for little Benjamin. At the time, Peinhaupt had sworn *Benjamin and not another one after him*, magic of the name Benjamin, as it were. Then came the twins, 360 euros each, because no group discount for twins, and so you come to exactly 340 euros times four, Peinhaupt calculated, as he slowly began to wonder why they'd left him waiting so long on the operating table. It's not exactly comfortable, either: first they get you to lie down—no one wants to lie there so exposed on the table—and then they disappear and leave you all alone. Please.

Four times 340 is 1,360, Peinhaupt calculated, which, subtracted from his net pay, left him with not even 700 euros. He would barely be getting by if it wasn't for the money he got paid under the table for serving court summonses. For the anesthesiologist's part, he could now take his time, because at 1,360, all doubt had been removed. He asked himself where the doctors had been this whole time. They finished prepping him for the procedure a few minutes ago, and then the light in the operating room went out. A minute later it came back on, but still no one had turned up. It occurred to him that he might have been lying under this harsh light for half an hour already waiting for the surgery, without a doctor anywhere in sight. *Is it possible they put me under already? Maybe I only dreamed that the lights went out briefly while they were prepping me, and the emergency generator started up.* Typical operation dream. You should know that Peinhaupt had declined the local anesthetic, and the Frau Doctor had said she suspected as much—fearful of even minor procedures, men tend to ask for general anesthesia. *It's not possible that the surgical team got scared off just because the power went out,* Peinhaupt thought, *it's all just a hysterical dream, and I'm already long under. And it's just my unconsciousness protesting against my most important body part's vitality getting snuffed out, hence the dream that the light went out.*

Suddenly Peinhaupt felt certain that everything must already be over. That he was just waking up in post-op, i.e., after a lucid nightmare. Because nothing else was possible, every other explanation was unthinkable. Peinhaupt could have been persuaded that it was the blade of the scalpel that was for holding and the handle for making the incision. The anesthesiologist must have really numbed him into a nightmare! *This just can't be real,* Peinhaupt decided.

Watch closely, Peinhaupt's lying there on the operating table nicely prepped like an inverse Adam, where the fig leaf is draped over his whole body except for where the fig leaf would cover Adam, when finally the door swings open, but it's not the anesthesiologist who opens the door, and it's not the urologist who comes in after him.

"Hey, Peinhaupt!"

And it wasn't even Frau Doctor Kressdorf who yelled out in shock, "Hey, Peinhaupt!" Whether you believe it or not. His two ex-colleagues Sykora and Zand. Zand, Erich! And Sykora! His old patrol buddies, walking through the door, completely dumbfounded and gawking at the exposed patient on the operating table, and they don't even laugh. In fact, Zand, Erich and Sykora seem petrified until Zand, Erich finally says, "Hey, Peinhaupt, what are you doing here?!"

CHAPTER 3

In retrospect, those seemed like the good old days to Frau Doctor Kressdorf. Like a carefree paradise. When she was still capable of getting worked up over a power outage or a water pipe breaking. When she still believed that a flooded clinic was reason enough to call the police. Or when a couple of cameras in the lobby had her running straight to the newspapers. And when, even in the middle of the power outage, it still occurred to her to call her driver before he got to Kitzbühel so he could relay everything to her husband.

She couldn't have known that her driver wasn't even on the autobahn yet. Only in hindsight did she realize that, at the exact time of the power outage, Herr Simon was still standing in the gas station convenience mart and having a quick double espresso.

Two gas station drunks were hanging out there, too, but Herr Simon, only coffee. Because first of all, as a chauffeur, no alcohol, and second of all, it didn't agree with the pills. Interesting, though. Since he'd stopped drinking alcohol, coffee had become all the more important to *Herr Simon*. He never would have dreamed of being called that back when he was still on the police force. But Kressdorf and the Frau

Doctor and everyone at the clinic referred to him that way, a service name, as it were.

Now don't go thinking that it bothered him, because: best job he'd had his whole life. Kressdorf's chauffeur, always meeting interesting people, you get the idea. Congressman Stachl, for example, who was just on the gas station's TV, on account of the morning news. Guaranteed that the gas station attendant and the two drunks didn't know him. The fatter of the two only laughed at the congressman's first name, because *Aurelius Stachl*, the fat drunk said, *a name like that's its own punishment*. But he definitely wouldn't have thought that Herr Simon might know Stachl personally. And not just know him, but know things about him. And he was overjoyed for Helena that her father had been given a chance with MegaLand because—college tuition, you can't start thinking too early about that, and you can't leave it all up to the Frau Doctor either. And one thing you can't forget. The clinic still wasn't completely out of debt, on account of the investments and the expenditures—don't even ask.

Nothing on the docket now except getting Helena to Kitzbühel. A glorious, sunny morning it was, and with his heart beating all the better from the espresso, he took those few steps from the gas station to the car with real attitude, like you might say, *life: perfectly okay*. When you think about what he was like a year ago, you've really got to say, hats off to the pills.

But when he saw that the car was empty, the pills had a hard time with him, of course. The double espresso stepped right into the foreground now because as he walked from the gas station to the BMW and didn't see Helena's head through the rear window, his heart stood still a moment, and then started pounding like he'd gulped down not just a double espresso but the contents of the entire coffee machine.

Interesting, though. His heart wasn't beating where the heart's supposed to beat, but in his head. Because his jugular must have been thicker than the fuel hose he'd gassed up the BMW with—*unbelievable, what a car like this guzzles*, but he told himself, *why should it bother me, I don't have to pay for it, and I'm too old for climate change.*

The blood was pumping so hard through his arteries and into his brain now that his entire head was throbbing like the time he'd held his ear right up to the speaker at a Jimi Hendrix concert in Stuttgart, 1969. They fit seven people in an old Citroën on the drive from Leitner's house to Stuttgart and back—eight of them, considering Leitner's girlfriend was already pregnant by the drive home. But she told them all it wasn't Hendrix's, no, it was Helmut Kögelberger's.

The hammering in his head was so loud that he didn't even hear the truck thundering down the street. And I do believe, even to this day, that it saved his life. Because he only noticed the truck after it had driven past him, i.e., too late to throw himself in front of its wheels. And maybe, given how much blood was shooting into his head, maybe that much more of the pills reached his brain. Because suddenly there was a straw to grasp at again, a glimmer of hope again, a silver lining again, in other words—*maybe I'm deceiving myself. Just because I can't see Helena's head through the back window when I'm fifteen feet away doesn't mean that she's not in the car anymore.*

Maybe she fell asleep and is just a little slouched down in her car seat, and that's why I don't see her, Herr Simon told himself. Which was complete nonsense, of course, when he knew for a fact that he should be able to see the child from here. Nor can a child really slouch if she's buckled correctly into her car seat, and Herr Simon never drove three feet without buckling Helena in according to the letter of the law—that you can't fairly accuse him of.

But by the next step, direction BMW, the blood in his head was already floating that last straw out to sea. *Who knows, maybe it's just a reflection in the back window.* There are so many cars today with tinted windows you can't even see through. And now he really did see something, or so it seemed. Helena had turned herself around in her car seat and was staring at him, deathly pale and with panic-stricken eyes. But it was only the reflection of his own face and the panic in his own eyes that caused Herr Simon to barely recognize himself. Now with conviction, another step and another step, but even from two steps away, still nothing of Helena to be seen. And as he stood directly beside the car, still nothing of Helena to be seen, not even through the side window. And when finally, with trembling fingers, he pressed the button on the car's key fob, it was of no use.

He kept pressing it, but the doors just unlocked and locked and unlocked and locked themselves, making that damned noise. Just once I'd like to understand how this remote-keyless-system actually works, because technology: a world of magic. Herr Simon was less interested in these sorts of things, he'd never had much of a grasp of technology, he used to get criticized for that all the time on the police force. A certain interest had awoken in him more recently since he'd become a chauffeur, because he'd counted himself fortunate a few times now to be living in an age when there are things that nobody would have dreamed of before, for example, unlocking a car from a distance like a magician. But now he had to accept that there was nothing magical about the key he was holding in his hand, because he could press and he could wish all he wanted, he could lock and unlock a thousand times, and he'd still only produce this knocking sound, like a drummer in a funeral march, driving the tears from the eyes of the mourners at the grave site. But for all that, the little girl, who the Frau Doctor had placed in his care, didn't pop back up.

Interesting, though. He must have blacked out at this point—missing footage, if you will. Because later he had no memory of how he had run around the gas station. He didn't remember running through the car wash. He didn't remember stumbling out of the lot and running up and down the street. He didn't remember running a second and then a third time around the gas station and through the car wash. Or better put, he did in fact remember it. But in reverse! Now how is something like this possible?

Watch closely. His forward-recollection kicked in only at the point when he ran back into the gas station. He doesn't mention a word about the child having disappeared, instead: *something's been stolen from my car*. Because otherwise the gas station attendant is going to call the police right away if he says *what* has been stolen. The police gave Herr Ex-Detective hell for that one. *Why didn't you call the police immediately, close off the streets, crackdowns, raids, the works!* And I do have to say, with something like this, you've simply got to call the police. Personal history with the police notwithstanding. Herr Simon made a big mistake there. Maybe the pills had him feeling a little too sure of himself. Even if afterward you can say ten times over, *it wouldn't have mattered anyway, there would've been no point in calling the police right away, because already far too late to close off the streets.* But he couldn't have known that. And at least he would have spared himself a little trouble. In hindsight. Above all he would have been spared those smartasses at the newspaper, because they managed to dig up from some channel or another his ancient police academy photo, and beneath it they put the caption: BODYGUARD SIPS SLOW DRIP BEFORE CALLING COPS.

Here I feel the need to add: that's not quite right, either! Because he only ordered his second cup of coffee in order to strike up a conversation with the gas station attendant now. Whether anything might have shown up on the surveillance monitors. The gas station attendant was very sociable, or really I should say cash register attendant, because attendants don't attend to the gas anymore these days, just the cash register. His name tag said *Milan*, and the young man explained to his customer in flawless German that the fuel pumps were surveilled, entrance surveilled, cash register surveilled, but over by the air pump, where Herr Simon had of course moved the car, not surveilled. But I have to say, this makes no sense, because an air pump can be stolen faster than a gas pump. But that's just how it was, and really, Herr Simon already knew as much, the first thing he'd done outside was look to see whether there was a camera in range.

"Can I maybe have a quick look anyway to see whether one of the other cameras picked up the thief getting away?"

"I'm afraid that's not allowed," Milan said and set his espresso down in front of him.

I don't know why, but—did he simply take a liking to Herr Simon, was he hoping for a good tip, did he have a guilty conscience that a theft had occurred on company property, or did Herr Simon just have a look of sheer desperation?—the attendant gestured for him to come behind the counter, and he showed him the flat monitor that hung above the cash register. Ten small cameras, if you can believe it: pump 1, pump 2, pump 3, pump 4, pump 5, pump 6, pump 7, pump 8, entrance, cash register.

Milan rewound the video and after just a few seconds you could see Herr Simon staggering backwards out of the shop, then running backwards around the gas station—you've got to picture this for yourself, you see yourself doing something that you just did five minutes ago but don't remember anymore—backwards into the car wash three times and backwards out three times, the greatest distress of his life looking ridiculous backwards and lasting just a few foolish seconds until, backwards, Herr Simon froze into a pillar of salt, as though Milan had paused the image. And a moment later, an entirely different Herr Simon walked leisurely backwards into the shop.

The attendant rewound the video to the place where Herr Simon was back at his car smiling, dirtying the clean windows, and taking his time sucking the gasoline out of the tank.

From that point on he played the video normally, i.e., forward and at the regular speed. And finally the scenes where Herr Simon was hoping to be able to see something suspicious. First you see him hanging the fuel nozzle back up. Then he moves the car so that the Volvo behind him can pull up. The Volvo driver gasses up, Herr Simon goes into the shop to pay, the Volvo drives off again without a stolen child. Then a silver Alfa pulls up to another pump, but the driver only walks out of the shop with two cans of Red Bull and no Helena. And briefly you see the red-haired woman—who was standing in Herr Simon's way as he was trying to balance his double espresso on the counter—walk into the shop. The attendant knows her, though, because she lives right across the street and was only buying something from the shop like she does every day. Then an old white Golf pulls through just because it wants to turn around, such that the license plate can't be made out, but it doesn't matter, because it didn't even come to a complete stop.

And then you see—forward this time and at the right speed—how Herr Simon comes back out of the shop and how he recoils as though the earth were opening up before him. It was almost worse for him to be experiencing this moment a second time now on-screen—or should I say for the first time.

"I'm sorry," Milan said. "You can't see anything. Was it valuable?"

"What?"

"What got stolen from your car?"

Herr Simon gave no answer. These forgotten minutes were such a nightmare that, if the screen had revealed him to be the kidnapper himself, he wouldn't have been surprised.

"Should I call the police?"

"It's too late now. They're already over the mountains."

He felt so numb that he had no idea what he should do. The pills weren't helping him, the coffee wasn't helping him, and the panic wasn't helping him. Instead, complete power outage.

"Give me another espresso," he said to Milan.

Because he was like a little kid now who's gotten into some trouble and thinks that nobody will find out about it if he just closes his eyes or hides behind the house. That the newspapers criticized him so much for it, though, I don't think is right, either. Somehow he expected two-year-old Helena to come strolling in through the door, and off they'd drive together. And believe it or not, he even bought a medium-sized chocolate bar for her. He told himself a medium-sized bar without any filling is a compromise that all parties could live with, chocolate proponents and chocolate opponents alike.

He ignored his cell phone's ringing. Or what's called ringing. Jimi Hendrix played "Castles Made of Sand" because that was what the son of the clinic's psychologist had conjured up for him his first week on the job. For the first time in his life, Jimi annoyed him because he was playing the same thing over and over. Herr Simon didn't even look at who was calling because the risk was too great that it might be the Frau Doctor. You should know, when he was on the road she would often check in during an abortion break to make sure everything was okay, and Herr Simon always made a point of asking Helena something so that her mama could hear her voice over the phone, and then she'd be pacified.

The two gas station drunks at the counter weren't

bothered any by the unrelenting ringtone either. Sure, they glanced over a little, but otherwise, no commentary. Fortunately, the gas station TV drowned out the cell phone a bit, too, because a blond newscaster was saying empathetic things to people with problems, but her voice was so aggressive that it sounded like the plastic surgeon had mistakenly nailed her vocal cords to her ears on her last visit.

Interesting customers came in now and then, which also distracted nicely. Because they didn't just come in and pay, but would make the rounds, too, a bottle of water, chips and a sleeve of cookies, sausage on a bun, a newspaper, there was a lot to look at, and meanwhile his cell phone would go off, maybe twice per customer. *And so castles made of sand fall in the sea, eventually*, Jimi sang again and again, but Herr Simon didn't pick up.

From the way the gas station customers ignored him, he realized that they simply took him for a gas station drunk himself. Because one thing you can't forget. Herr Simon looked like he'd just been to hell and back.

"Your phone's ringing," a customer said on her way out, on account of the way he was staring at her. But she couldn't have known that it was only because of the chocolate bar she'd bought. He ordered himself another espresso, and when Helena still didn't turn up, he left. Maybe she'd climbed back into the car, maybe she'd just gone on a little outing, and now she was back in her car seat again. Or another possibility. Maybe Herr Simon had just hallucinated the whole thing, possibly due to the pills? Because he did have a nonalcoholic beer yesterday, and even in nonalcoholic beer there's still a little bit of alcohol, which means, if you drink thirty-six:

drunken stupor. He'd only had one, but still, hope is hope. Or another possibility altogether: the kidnappers had changed their minds. They had returned the child, acting as if it had been nothing. Or, anti-abortionist Knoll had only wanted to make a slight threat, taking the child away briefly, like he'd threatened the Frau Doctor before, and then giving her right back—a rapping at the window, as it were.

Herr Simon retraced his steps exactly as he had taken them before, maybe out of a certain superstition that repeating the previous experience would make it un-happen. But when it comes to superstition, the good lord is merciless, he hates it like a CEO does a labor union. And still no Helena through the back window, still no Helena through the side window, still no Helena when he pressed the button on the key fob, and from the driver's seat, still no Helena in the rearview mirror. At that moment, as he looked in the rearview mirror, his cell phone went off again. It made Herr Simon so furious that he pounded his fist on the steering wheel. Because he imagined the ringtone scaring Helena away, as though if it weren't for Jimi Hendrix maybe she'd be sitting there in the rearview mirror. *And so castles made of sand fall in the sea*, Jimi sang like he was mocking him, *eventually*.

Because of the fist-pounding and the third espresso, his heart was throwing another tantrum. But he forced himself to search the car. You're going to say, *where's she supposed to be, Helena, she's not hiding beneath the hood*. But you see how the shock was slowly driving him mad. The panic was enough to drive him crazy, and where the panic left off, the pills picked up and drove him even crazier. Because now he was clinging to the thought that children like to hide. That it's fun for kids, you get the idea. And even though the little girl wouldn't have been in a position to hide anywhere but her car seat, he searched the whole car. Maybe she was curled up comfortably behind the backseat, waiting for that dumb driver to finally find her. But no Helena behind the seats, no Helena under the seats, no Helena in the glove compartment, no Helena beneath the floor mats, not even a Helena in the trunk.

There was a moment when Herr Simon thought he might start crying. But it didn't come from within, not from his inner desperation, no, it came more from his face, from outside. And even then he didn't cry. Instead, whether you believe it or not: he sneezed five times in a row. By the fifth time he was already walking back through the gas station's automatic doors and ordering himself another espresso. And then finally he called Kressdorf. The Frau Doctor, impossible, he'd rather die, because to tell a mother *I lost your child*. In a situation like that you fear the mightiest Lion of Construction less than you do the mother.

At first he just stared a while at Kressdorf's number and wondered, *should I or shouldn't I?* But then, finally, he dialed. And immediately hung up again before it even started ringing. And then, finally, he dialed and actually waited for it to ring, too.

CHAPTER 4

Kressdorf always had to laugh when people referred to him as a Lion of Construction. Even his wife sometimes said to him, "Good thing I didn't know at the time what a *Lion of Construction* you were." Otherwise, he wouldn't have had a chance with her, because when they were first starting out, she had someone more along the lines of an architect in mind for herself.

Kressdorf was amused by this, and in fact he'd been thinking just the opposite, *good thing she didn't realize that I was still a nobody back then.* Because he was paying off those bouquets of roses on his credit card for years. Most people think a Lion of Construction gets his start with the larger contractors. These days if you plunk your first single-family house down on a field and it doesn't collapse by the end of the day, instant Construction Lion. And Kressdorf, unfortunately, had been spinning his wheels, trying to get somewhere for years. He was nearly forty when he met the med student, and even by then, he still couldn't really afford the expensive hotels.

His rise to the top only really began with the cabin in the Kitzbühel mountains. You should know, without cabins you don't come into contracts. Mountain houses, ski lodges, today they teach you that in business school, but Kressdorf had to figure it all out on his own, and it took him the first half of his career. But once he did, he took all the money he'd earned in those first twenty years and put it into a real Kitzbühel throat-slitter—all for a cabin that was completely rotted out, only thing holding it together were the woodworms. And then, of course, bank directors, politicians, journalists, bishops, investors—suddenly they were all eating out of his hand. But I should add: a cabin isn't a cabin isn't a cabin. Because a tasteful mountain palace like the one Kressdorf had magically whipped up out of the woodworm dump—that had the small-town mayors lining up for years, and just to nab an appointment to throw back a quick schnapps with him.

But no mayors these days, of course, because only the innermost circle, i.e., high-level power meetings. Today there were only three of them sitting in the hunter's den. Well, purely from their perspective. The girls were still upstairs sleeping, since it had gone on a bit late the night before, so they said, *we'll let them sleep in a little today*.

The mood was terribly peaceful, and as Bank Director Reinhard remarked, "A day like this without a cell phone is like two weeks' vacation with a cell phone." Congressman Stachl nodded in such emphatic agreement that the flakes from his black beard went scattering, on account of neurodermatitis. But don't go thinking that Congressman Stachl was just a generally emphatic nodder. Quite the opposite: Bank Director Reinhard's cell phone ban annoyed him, but so that Reinhard wouldn't pick up on this, he nodded emphatically—camouflage, if you will. But the neurodermatitis, of course, wasn't about to let itself be mistaken for something it wasn't, and so the congressman couldn't stop scratching his beard. A night at the cabin always had him itching four times as much, and then the itching would just annoy him all the more, i.e., catch-22. Just so you don't get the wrong idea about where the fine layer of dust covering Aurelius Stachl's side of the wooden table came from.

Bank Director Reinhard, on the other hand. For him, one would have to invent the word "relaxed," if it didn't already exist. And I don't just mean his paunch, which is often a point of confusion, and maybe his pleasant stoutness only got to be that stout because it's got so many people in the deep freezer that it can't keep up with the leftovers. But the strange thing about Reinhard was that he didn't look fat, even though he was definitely hiding fifty, sixty kilos too many under his black turtleneck sweater. It wasn't accredited against him, though. For a man of sixty, he looked more like a portly high school student who's way ahead of everyone in school, except in gym class. He's always so comfortably enthroned upon his chair, looking out from the thick lenses of the glasses perched on his plump face, but managing somehow to look imposing. And believe it or not, when the girls were brought in last night, you could tell right away that they preferred Reinhard over Stachl, even though Stachl is half as old, athletic, tall, and slim, a real gladiator compared to Reinhard. And it definitely wasn't because of the flaking skin on his face, either, because his beard covered it very well. But with Reinhard maybe instinctually the girls sensed something more benevolent, paternal.

And I can honestly say, in the mountains he truly was.

He transformed into a benevolent person there. I don't know if it was because of the altitude, the quietude, or simply the hunting. Reinhard himself marveled at how relaxed he always was in the mountains. That's why he liked coming up here so much. Day to day he had to forcibly suppress his benevolent side. What do you think would become of the bank if he were to direct it with his hunting benevolence?

But Reinhard, of course, was a far too responsible person for that. He'd directed the bank very successfully for twenty years—hundreds, if not thousands, of young bank girls would have lost their jobs if Reinhard hadn't done his so well. Then there was his own family in Klosterneuburg, always present at every birthday, all four kids. He even volunteered at the church when time permitted; above all, when his wife permitted, of course. Many people have wondered how Reinhard does it all. But it's precisely because he's so good at relaxing. And he hadn't been as relaxed as he was today in a long time.

"That was a grand idea you had, banning cell phones here in the mountains," he said to Kressdorf, and he smiled so contentedly that his beady eyes nearly disappeared completely behind the thick lenses of his glasses.

In truth, of course, it had been Bank Director Reinhard's own idea. His express wish: no cell phones, not just out hunting but in the cabin, too. Because they still always called it a "cabin," even though Kressdorf had built it into a full-fledged mountain lodge. *No cell phones in the cabin*, Reinhard said, *because that's why we go: to be in nature*. My god, a bank manager like him has an enormous amount of responsibility, he's allowed to indulge in a little extra amusement now and then, a little humiliation on the side, by praising someone for an idea that had been forced on him. It's a behavior related on many levels to this thing where you have to thank the person who slaps you in the face, but much friendlier, because no slap in the face, only praise. If he wanted something, all Reinhard had to do was whisper and everyone would immediately jump, and afterward he'd say, *that was a grand idea you had.*

Kressdorf wasn't bothered by this. But Congressman Stachl was. He turned red every time Reinhard praised him like a little boy for something he hadn't done. But Kressdorf only saw the big picture, i.e., the big contract. Because for a project like MegaLand, even a Lion of Construction can let a good-natured sadist have his fun and accept his praise for a cell phone ban that he himself imposed. And one thing you can't forget: it was a project he would've jumped at all over again, just like he had back when he bought the cabin with his last few bucks.

"I could watch that rabbit for hours," Bank Director Reinhard said smiling, his stout minister's mouth beaming with satisfaction. And for my part: *I could watch that Reinhard smile for hours.* There was something about watching the animals feeding that was so peaceful to him that it had almost meant more to him than the hunt itself these past few years. And sometimes Stachl would even whisper blasphemously from behind a cupped hand: *Reinhard doesn't even like to shoot anymore, the animals behind the glass are enough for him.*

You should know, a glass panel separated the hunters' den from the rabbit pen. It's all the rage these days with cabins, and it was Kressdorf who originally invented it. He'd had the glass wall installed with his last bit of cash at the time. But when *Hunting Review* did a multipage photo spread of his innovative idea, everyone copied it immediately, of course. Basically, this glass panel between the hunters' den and the stables formed the basis of the whole Kressdorf empire, because people liked it, you wouldn't believe. He hadn't even demonstrated the one-way-mirror-at-the-press-of-a-button for them. No, just the plain glass function got people excited. So you'd be eating your bacon in the hunters' den, drinking your schnapps, counting your millions, fondling your ill-gotten gains, and through the glass panel, you could watch the animals in their innocent animal existence. Interesting, though. Reinhard wasn't amused one bit when Congressman Stachl made a joke about the bunnies behind the glass. Because that was too vulgar for Reinhard. He expected a certain *niveau* from a congressman, even at the cabin.

Now that it was morning, the girls weren't in the rabbit pen anymore, anyway. They slept till noon, which was a foreign world to Reinhard. He'd never understood sleeping in, because the morning was the most beautiful time of day for him, and every morning at six sharp: the five Tibetans.

"You'll have to excuse me, I'll just be a moment . . ." Reinhard said to Kressdorf and pulled out his cell phone. Because that was the most important part of the deal, of course, that Reinhard should get to make at least one brief call, lifting the very ban, as it were, that Kressdorf supposedly had enacted. But always with contrite apology. Congressman Stachl had never dared, he just pretended he had diarrhea and made his important phone calls from the bathroom every five minutes.

And so, while Reinhard was on the phone in the hunters' den, Stachl went to the bathroom again and turned his phone back on. Beneath his thick black hair his head was riddled with scars, one for every time it had bumped into the low ceiling in the cabin's bathroom. At his height he couldn't stand fully upright in there, and the congressman was a nervous telephoner as it was, fidgeting and gesticulating. Maybe his pent-up resentment toward Reinhard played a part, too, in him regularly hitting his head in the bathroom. If not on the window latch or the light fixture then on the deer rack or the cabinet that stored the toilet paper. Especially when a call startled him, he was at risk. Typical example: just now he forgot to stoop down on his way out the door. The text message had something to do with it, guaranteed. Because: emergency. Kressdorf's wife couldn't get hold of her husband and it was urgent for him to call her.

CHAPTER 5

"Now she's given up," one of the two gas station drunks said. The thin one, because the fat one was standing with his back to Herr Simon, but he had such a belly that his back brushed up against the neighboring table. And so you can see just how badly things were going for the chauffeur. That he hadn't even noticed that his cell phone had been completely silent for ten minutes. You should know, when he still couldn't get hold of Kressdorf after three tries, he gave up. And I suspect he only tried in the first place because he knew about the cell phone ban, and so it would have been a huge coincidence if Kressdorf had picked up. But Herr Simon didn't turn off his cell phone after his pointless attempts, either. Instead he remained snug in that painful middle ground, without a solution and without any refuge, ergo triggering "Castles Made of Sand." But when it suddenly stopped, it didn't strike him as suspicious. It pains me when I think how slow his brain was compared to the gas station drunks, who noticed it before he did.

"Mine calls all day, too," the thin one announced, loudly enough for the gas station attendant to hear it, too, from where he was putting away a stack of frozen Napoli pizzas in the refrigerated cases. "I don't know what it is with women."

Herr Simon took advantage of the gas station attendant's

brief glance over to point to his empty cup. And the gas station attendant gave a nod as if to say: *I'll just quickly put away the pizza boxes so that they don't start thawing, and then I'll bring you another espresso.*

"That they have to have their beaks flapping all day long," the thin one said.

"Tee tee tee tee tee tee tee!" the beer belly said in a high-pitched voice and made a motion like a bird's beak with his chubby little left hand, a babbling goose, as it were.

"Not picking up's the only thing that helps sometimes," the thin one said. "Right, Milan?"

"Tee tee tee tee tee tee tee!" went the beer belly. I don't know why the beer belly had such a high-pitched voice, presumably the female hormones in hops, and if you're a man then you get breasts and a high-pitched voice, but what would be interesting is whether that's true for nonalcoholic beer, too.

As he walked past, Milan said, "Your wife's always on the phone with her boyfriend. Yugo-lover!"

The thin one laughed because he didn't have a wife anyway, so the comment couldn't really be taken as an insult, and in fact, was even very nice of Milan, who otherwise didn't give the thin one an answer very often because when you're a gas station attendant, your head grows weary of your gas station drunks over the course of the day.

"Tee tee tee tee tee tee tee!" went the belly-talker's sausage fingers again. It had definitely been fifteen minutes already since Jimi Hendrix last sang, and Herr Simon still didn't think anything of it. When Milan came with the espresso, the chauffeur asked him, "And your wife? What's her name?"

"What's your wife's name?" Milan asked, smirking, and passed the question along to the thin one.

"Angelina Jolie." The thin guy looked as serious as if he were providing the name of his wife to the emergency room at the hospital.

"Heidi Klump." The fat one was quick to introduce his wife, too.

Herr Simon didn't laugh, though. "The woman on the surveillance tape," he pressed Milan. "The red-haired one who shops here every day."

"No clue. She lives right over there. I always see her going into that house. But her name, no idea. She often comes in twice a day and buys—"

What she buys, Herr Simon didn't catch. But that you can't criticize him for, because it was drowned out by the forceful shouts and by the loud clattering of the CD rack and the box of lighters and the flashlight special and the lottery ticket dispenser and the keychains, all crashing to the floor.

He shouldn't have overlooked the fact that his cell phone had been silent the whole time he'd been in the bathroom. The gas station's bathroom, *picobello*, immaculate, that never happens—but pay attention, Herr Simon had left his cell phone lying out on the table, didn't think anything of it and when he came back from the bathroom it wasn't ringing anymore. So it's almost his unconsciousness that you have to find fault with. Every human being has secret desires, don't ask, and it's possible he just wanted to be caught finally, possible he even wished for it somewhere in the very back of his head, yearned for the fat drunk to seize the opportunity and pick up the phone on a lark while he was in the bathroom.

Herr Simon wasn't angry at the gas station drunk for it afterward. On the contrary, he even invited him out after the funeral. He was only mad at himself, and I should add that, for someone who used to be on the police force, there's reason not to be purely happy in a situation where your cell phone stops pestering you. Because when relentless phone terrorizing has been going on for more than an hour and suddenly comes to a stop, you have to ask yourself why. It's like how if your spouse stops nagging you, then you know he's cheating on you. And if the parents of your kidnapped child stop calling, then you know they've got you.

It was only at that moment when the police officer was behind him, grabbing him between the legs in a brutal manner, that Herr Simon realized amid his shriek of pain that he hadn't understood the officer's question correctly, even though he had yelled it into his ear: "Where have you got the kid?"

I tell you, though, at that second Peinhaupt wasn't exactly in prime condition to receive an immediate answer. No, he had a scandal to defuse that his two colleagues—who were securing the escape routes, Zand, Erich the gas station entrance and Sykora the back exit—had surprised him with on the sterilization table that fateful morning. After the creepy phone call with the gas station drunk, the clinic director's panic became Peinhaupt's chance at redemption, of course. And so maybe you grab on all the more doggedly, even though you don't realize yet that you're standing right behind the biggest case of your life.

CHAPTER 6

It belongs to the less sympathetic side of human beings that the anger felt toward one person should get taken out on another. You kick over your beer bottle because you got a sausage that's more casing than meat. You yell at your wife because your mistress asked a stupid question. Or you blame the detective because the child entrusted to you got kidnapped from your car.

As an ex-cop himself, Herr Simon had to know that Peinhaupt was only doing his job. Peinhaupt had to whether he wanted to or not. Sure, he was a little over zealous with the interrogation, that's obvious. After the disgrace in the operating room, of course, two-hundred-percent bull, don't even ask. He snapped the case right up, and every single word out of Peinhaupt had a harshness and a consequence, as if it were shooting straight from his intact spermatic cord at the last possible second, i.e., the empire was fighting back.

It was driving Herr Simon crazy, how much time Peinhaupt was squandering by using the fact that he hadn't called sooner against him. Because—old chestnut—everything in the world would only take half as long, all work would go three times as fast, if there wasn't always a man needing to prove that he was one. Just look at Peinhaupt. With the energy he spent shaking down the chauffeur, he could have sired ten new Helenas. But the one who this was all about, he'd lost sight of a little.

At least that's how it came across to Herr Simon. Because, fourth round of questioning already—hourlong interrogation after the arrest, the interrogation last night, the interrogation this morning, and now, instead of lunch, more grilling. As an ex-cop, of course, he waas coming from the know-it-all's point of view—law of nature, as it were. And to be perfectly honest, he even criticized the police for wasting their time with him instead of going after the kidnappers, but he wasn't exactly helping matters, either, with his stubborn insistence that the interrogation get its show on the road and fast. Because when a person has a guilty conscience, most of the time he just makes everything worse. So, out of a guilty conscience—and sheer man-versus-man—Herr Simon gave the longest speech of his life.

"You've asked me three times now whether I locked the car, and I've told you three times, yes, locked. And before you fritter away any more time, I'll go ahead and say it a fourth time: the car was locked! Not open! Closed! I learned in the police academy, too, that *Verhör* comes from *verhören*, but . . ."

I should explain briefly what all that with the *verhören* was about. Because, old interrogation trick—act like you *mishear*, or *verhören*, the first time. So if somebody says the car was locked, then five minutes later in the interrogation, or *Verhör*, you act like he said it wasn't locked. Inside police joke: *Verhör* comes from *verhören*. So Herr Simon was offended, of course, that Peinhaupt came at him with that old stunt. He couldn't have known what Peinhaupt had gone through yesterday, or else maybe he wouldn't have given such a long speech just now.

"And now you can ask me five more times," he—I need to quickly add here—shouted, "whether I noticed anyone following me, and I'll tell you five more times, nobody followed me. And you can ask me ten more times why I didn't gas up the night before, and I'll tell you ten more times, I don't know, it was an oversight, there were no bad intentions, just like there are no bad intentions on your end, trotting out pointless questions here for all of eternity, instead of searching for the child. No, you just can't do any better."

"And the car was locked?" Peinhaupt asked blankly and shot him a stupid look, like a man might look at a woman after saying to her for the third time: *and you're completely sure that we're better off going to my place instead of yours.* Even though she's already told him twice, *leave me alone, you jackass.*

Herr Simon wasn't honestly sure himself whether the car—before he locked and unlocked it a thousand times—had been locked in the first place. But, locked or unlocked, that makes about as much of a difference to a criminal as a bullet entertaining the question of which SPF sunscreen you've got on as it bores its way into your forehead.

"Leave me alone, you jackass," he answered Peinhaupt.

Because he knew perfectly well that for Peinhaupt it wasn't about whether the car was locked. That much he still remembered from his own police days, how you'd make a big deal out of something insignificant for hours, and then slip in the crucial question completely off the cuff. Not unlike death, which, more often than not, will pick you up for skin cancer on account of an old sunburn, and so you see once again how sunscreen's more important than ducking bullets your whole life.

Now, what was it that Peinhaupt was going to casually ask the suspicious chauffeur? How well he knew Knoll, of course. But there was no way of posing the question of the pro-life boss himself without making everything immediately obvious. How often Herr Simon had seen Knoll. Whether he'd ever spoken with him. What he made of the threats that Knoll had issued against the Frau Doctor.

"Why didn't you just ask me that from the beginning?" Herr Simon yelled. I have to say, I hardly recognize him like this. It's my suspicion that the pills were now to blame for his sudden aggression. "Why have you been screwing around here this whole time with whether I saw someone in the rearview mirror or whether the car was locked?"

"Or why you didn't call us right away."

"Or why I didn't call you right away. Maybe I was in shock, or maybe—"

"Maybe you were in cahoots with Knoll."

"If you're so certain that Knoll's behind it, why don't you just go pick up the kid from him?"

The detective made a dopey face, as if to say, *like we're going to tell you of all people what we're doing with Knoll right now.*

"Well now, someone's in an awful hurry all of the sudden, Herr Simon."

"Where would I know Knoll from? You know for a fact that Knoll doesn't stand there himself in front of the abortion clinic."

He was right on that account, of course. Knoll didn't personally stand in the street and try to prevent patients from entering the clinic with his own hands. You don't ever do something like that yourself! A bank director like Reinhard doesn't personally carry the TV out of the house when someone defaults on a loan, either. Knoll had enough church-types to stand in front of the clinic for him all day with rapt expressions on their faces and holding photos of embryos up in the air with the word "Murder" written across them.

"Just how am I, of all people, supposed to have kidnapped Helena?"

"Egypt's third president was assassinated by his own bodyguard."

"I wasn't hired to be a bodyguard. I was hired to be a driver!"

Peinhaupt reached for the telephone and called up front to see whether the Frau Doctor was in the building. That sent Herr Simon into a panic—you'd have thought Peinhaupt had called in the bloodhounds.

"I'm just a driver," he said, so sheepishly that he held himself in contempt.

"The Frau Doctor told us she and her husband selected you from a large number of candidates because of your police background."

"So what?"

"So what. So that's exactly why you were more than just a driver, Herr Simon. Do you think, with the threat being as great as it was, that they would have entrusted their child to just any stranger?"

You should know, back before Herr Simon had been hired, Knoll once said to the Frau Doctor during an argument that she should watch out for her only child so that the good lord doesn't make *her* child disappear—like all those children she'd taken away from the good lord.

"Anti-abortionists don't kidnap! They're just poor crazies, slinging their rosaries. The anti-abortionists aren't *anti*-children—they're *pro*-children!"

"And the threats from Knoll you simply didn't take seriously. Maybe you know him so well that you can assess his character that accurately?"

"He'd be the first kidnapper to announce the kidnapping ahead of time."

"Don't play any dumber than you already are. That's exactly what's so funny about it. If a kidnapper wants to extort money, then naturally he's not going to announce it beforehand. But if he has a higher purpose, that's something else altogether."

"So that's what you learn at the police academy these days?"

"As long as the kidnapper doesn't make contact, then the demand is from Knoll to shut down the clinic, the only lead we've got anyway. And it can be assumed that a desperate mother like the Frau Doctor will grasp at any available straw. The longer the kidnapper's silent, the more weight's given to Knoll's old demand. Without even having to send word. And no ransom to be handed over, either. A kidnapping without a neuralgic point, my dear Simon."

I have to say, Knoll's plan wouldn't have been half bad. First, the casually made threat, without any witnesses in the room, of course, and not too long thereafter, the kidnapping. Because there's nothing worse for the family than a kidnapping where no demand is made. And nothing worse for the police than a kidnapping where no ransom is handed over. As soon as the Frau Doctor closes the clinic on her own initiative without the kidnapper having to make a single call, the kid will turn back up safe and sound. Coincidence.

"Then it's Knoll you're after and not me. I've never seen the man before."

"A woman's waiting outside for you," Peinhaupt said with a smirk and handed him the protocol to sign.

But his signature looked like two-year-old Helena had scrawled it for her driver. His hand trembled so much out of fear of her mother that Doctor Parkinson himself would have been proud of Herr Simon.

CHAPTER 7

Good news now. It wasn't the Frau Doctor who was waiting for Herr Simon outside in the hallway. She had enough to deal with, what with her nervous breakdown. Instead, Natalie was sitting out on the bench and looking at him with those serious eyes of hers that Herr Simon had liked from day one. Pay attention: Natalie was the clinic's psychologist, because a pregnancy's never terminated without psychological counseling. And it was the psychologist, of all people, who got to experience an unwelcome side effect of the pills in his first week on the job. You should know, the pills made him a little volatile. He'd often be serenity personified, then something small would set him off all over again. Or, he'd let a stupid joke rip that never would've even occurred to him before. Just so you understand. Because Natalie was very hurt at the time, even though Herr Simon hadn't meant anything bad by it. It was just a careless moment when he'd played dumb and pretended like he thought her job was to counsel the embryos: dispensing consolation along the lines of, *don't make a big deal of it, life's not that popular anyway, rest assured you can do without it, be glad that you can keep flying with the gnats*.

Maybe you've already noticed how much he liked Natalie,

because men don't talk like such imbeciles otherwise. Did he get off on the wrong foot with Natalie? Don't even ask. He tallied it up afterward, and believe it or not, she'd used the word "puberty" three times in one sentence.

And Herr Simon managed to insult her a second time within the same week. But to that I have to say, Natalie was being overly sensitive! Because she didn't necessarily have to rebuff his compliment—that, in her case, it would have been a pity if she hadn't been brought into this world—with such a scowl. My god, there will always be people who'll make you want to say, it wouldn't have been such a pity if their mothers had thought elsewise, and then for the vast majority, you'd say, it wouldn't have made a difference one way or another whether they're here or not—neutral, as it were. But very rarely is there a person who makes you say, it would've been an outright shame. See Natalie, with her black curls, with her white teeth, with her green specks in her dark-brown eyes, and with her mouth, which, in a single sentence, used the word "puberty" three times. But if you work in an area like the one Natalie works in, of course you don't want to hear such a dubious compliment. I can understand Natalie on that. On the other hand, Herr Simon was brand new in the workplace at the time, he had yet to adopt the right conversational tone for the clinic, because—always a particular knowledge set, what you're allowed to say where and how, and what you're not allowed to say how and where.

But despite this minor friction, I don't wish to say that Natalie didn't like Herr Simon. Quite the opposite! Although she knew nothing of his police past, she'd felt right away that behind the slightly stiff and straitlaced chauffeur, an entirely different person was hiding. Because you can't fool a skilled psychologist with the Herr Simon routine when really you're an old Brenner.

But it was jinxed for these two, because today they were back on the rocks all over again.

"My god, look at you!" they both said at the same time.

And if it hadn't been so sad, maybe they would have laughed and could have possibly begun a love story with this simultaneous exclamation, but alas, it was only a death story.

Well, death story only in the long run, what with all that happened the next week and the dirt that got dredged up, television, newspaper, and, and, and. Short term, as long as they were sitting there on the bench in the police station, no death story, of course, no, just an eviction story. Watch closely: Natalie had his possessions in a cheap duffel bag, and she got him to hand over his car keys and his key to the chauffeur's apartment. Because Kressdorf had built a modest chauffeur's quarters above the double garage in the driveway to the Hietzinger villa—quite comfortable—but not Herr Simon's apartment anymore now because the Frau Doctor said, *I never want to see that man again*. You see, she was almost more afraid of him than he was of her.

Natalie handed him an envelope containing one month's pay, and then she offered him her hand in farewell, and said something terribly nice that pained Herr Simon more than if she'd called him a murderer. Listen closely. She said, "Herr Simon, Helena always liked you."

"I'll find those filthy—" he said, but his voice wobbled so much on "filthy" that he couldn't get "pigs" out.

Natalie understood him regardless, though. She gave

him a disapproving look just like she used to do, and shook her head in warning, as if to say: *don't make things any worse, Herr Simon.*

This treatment was preferable to him just now, though, because he'd calmed himself down enough to ask in a normal voice, "Have the kidnappers made any demands yet?"

"Herr Simon," Natalie said, and pressed her lips so thin that a kiss would have been perilous.

"In a situation like this a private investigator can find a child much quicker."

"Herr Simon!"

"It'll take the police three weeks just to find someone competent, by then he'll be out sick, and after that they'll say: 'Now it's too late, statute of limitations.'"

"Herr Simon, listen carefully to me. You're not to undertake anything in this case." She looked at him so seriously with her dark eyes that everything else receded from view. "We know that you used to be on the police force."

Naturally she felt the need to emphasize this because until recently she was the only one who didn't know. "But you're not on the force anymore," the psychologist said, professional brainwashing, as it were. "You have feelings of guilt, but you're not allowed to solve this case with your own fists."

"I'm not talking about fists," he said, "but—"

"We're not talking about absolutely anything, Herr Simon. Or else, the child might be brought into only greater danger. The police have already taken the matter in hand."

"Have the kidnappers made contact at all?"

"The detectives will take care of it."

"Strange. Kidnappers almost always demand no police.

And these are demanding exactly the opposite: just police, no Brenner."

"No Brenner," Natalie said, earnestly and with that certain air of superiority that only people who know they're doing the right thing get. But one thing to jot down for your own life. Certainty: always black ice. And Natalie didn't realize the huge mistake she'd just made. Because that was the first time she didn't call him "Herr Simon," but rather "Brenner."

And it struck Brenner that, in doing so, she was authorizing him to undertake the investigation. Unconsciously, as it were.

CHAPTER 8

Thirty hours after the girl's disappearance, Brenner was back at large. Outside it was raining, and later on he'd often think about how the moment he set foot on the street, what shot through his head were the words "Zone of Transparency." Because let's be honest with each other, a normal person wouldn't think "Zone of Transparency" when he walked out of the police station and into the rain ten times and saw on his watch that the mishap occurred exactly thirty hours ago.

The rain, by and large, had never bothered Brenner much, and when the windshield wipers were doing their job well it was always calming, meditative for him. Helena was completely in love with the windshield wipers anyway, often he'd switch them on briefly even in the nicest weather just to delight her. But when you're a chauffeur without a car who's standing in the rain, then, subjectively speaking of course, that's the moment when it hits you that you're having a crisis. And the colossal duffel bag wasn't exactly making things any easier.

You should know by now: crisis always equals opportunity! And before you start feeling sorry for Brenner—how he stood there in the rain without a car and without a job and without an apartment and without an umbrella and without a plan and with only this cheap duffel bag and this nuisance of a brainworm, "Zone of Transparency"—there's one thing I need to tell you: if it hadn't been raining, if Brenner weren't so depressed walking in the rain, as if he'd never heard of a bus or a train or a taxi, he might never have noticed.

When a man follows you for a while in the rain, at some point you ask yourself, why is he doing that? Add to that, when the man, like Brenner, has no umbrella, but unlike Brenner, not a single hair. Total baldness might even be an advantage in the rain, because at least you don't have wet hair afterward. But Brenner's shadower was bald in such an old-fashioned way, with a wreath of hair around his head, i.e., the worst kind in the rain, because the raindrops hammer away at the unprotected bald part, and regardless, wet hair.

The aggravating presence of his shadower pulled Brenner out of his lethargy a little. To this day I don't know what aggravated him more: that they still held him suspect and had him shadowed, or that baldy was such a dilettante about it.

And there you have it, once again, the best proof that there's nothing in the world that doesn't also have its good side. Because your average Viennese citizen might find it depressing that a new off-track betting parlor opens up every day, but purely for detective street practices, it's convenient when you can wait in the entrance of the next betting parlor for your shadower.

"Next time, wear a sign that says 'Shadowing'!" Brenner advised his trusty stalker, who nearly ran smack into him. "Then maybe you'd be less conspicuous."

And not just his face, of course, but his whole bald head, too, turned red, only his lips were white as they said, "I need to speak with you."

"There are easier ways to go about it."

"I wanted to make sure that we weren't being shadowed."

And at that moment, as the man offered him his hand, it occurred to Brenner where he'd read the heading "Zone of Transparency."

"Sebastian Knoll," the man chipperly introduced himself.

I don't know if it was because of the sleepless night in the holding cell at the police station, or simply the state of shock Brenner had been in for thirty hours now, that could explain why he suddenly had the feeling he'd better hold on tight to the door frame to keep himself from sinking into a fever dream.

In the green light of the betting parlor's neon sign, he could see all too clearly the large raindrops crawling through Knoll's wreath of hair. The purple spider veins on his earlobe, from an ancient piercing that had since closed up, looked to Brenner like a cryptic sign of either a cult or something extraterrestrial. Through the open door, racehorses and race dogs and race cars could be seen flickering across a TV screen. Outside, an unnaturally red streetcar sailed elegantly through the spray of rain, and above the door the ventilation system whooshed with the placing of bets, while just a few centimeters in front of Brenner, the dripping wet face of Knoll, the abortion fanatic, was claiming he must urgently speak with him.

Brenner wasn't really listening to him, though, because the moment Knoll said his name it occurred to him that one of Knoll's activists had shoved a brochure into his hand a few weeks ago in which he'd read the heading "Zone of Transparency."

Pay attention: that's what the glassy membrane of the ovum is called, into which the sperm implants itself—science, as it were. And believe it or not, for that first cell to divide: it takes thirty hours exactly. While the bald-headed man's voice got increasingly impatient, from the betting commotion and the ventilation system drowning him out, Brenner couldn't fight the thought that, exactly thirty hours after Helena's disappearance, a chain reaction was now being set into motion. Just like the automatic sequence depicted so nicely in the brochure, how day after day the cells divide, and divide again, and divide again, without any human intervention. Suddenly he felt certain—or did it just seem that way to him in retrospect, what with the full knowledge one acquires in retrospect—that for anti-abortionist Knoll to turn up exactly thirty hours after the child's disappearance was a sign that catastrophe would only multiply as automatically as cell division itself, just not in the direction of life. Rather, in the opposite direction.

"You're Knoll?"

Interesting, though. Just now Brenner noticed that the entrance to the betting parlor was also surveilled with a camera. You can understand why they'd surveil it, because a betting parlor attracts a certain kind of person. Surveillance cameras were such a sore spot for Brenner, though, that he pinned this cheap dummy right on Knoll's shoulders, even though there was no Sectec logo on it like on the cameras in the clinic. Well, figuratively pinned it on his shoulders, because very calmly he said, "I've always heard that Knoll never reveals himself, that he just pulls strings from the background."

And just to escape the camera, Brenner went inside the betting parlor and sat down at the first empty table he saw. He ordered an espresso. Knoll ordered a hot tea, because he was afraid of catching a chill in his wet clothes. And when the drinks came, he said, "I'm sure you've heard quite a bit about me. But, the things that get said about people aren't true most of the time, you know. Things have been said about you, too, which I hope aren't true."

The arrogance with which he said this rubbed Brenner entirely the wrong way. But he couldn't help but like how modestly Knoll wiped his bald head dry with the small napkin placed between his tea cup and saucer.

"Now I finally know what these doilies are good for," Knoll said, grinning. "Otherwise, they stick so badly to the bottom of your cup that you wonder what the point of them is. If you don't spill, you don't need them, and if you do spill, they just spread the mess farther."

"What do you want from me?"

Knoll balled up the napkin, but instead of putting it in the ashtray, he slipped it as inconspicuously as possible into his pocket, like someone who doesn't like to leave any trace behind.

"I'd like to see the Kressdorf kid returned as quickly as possible."

"Talking to me is only going to make you look more suspicious to the police," Brenner said. "Besides, I just got taken off of it."

"It'll look much the same to the good Frau Doctor. Fired! Without even batting an eye at employment law, of course."

"Yeah, well. Gross negligence is reason enough."

"They'll always find something!"

Knoll had such an inscrutable smile on his lips that Brenner wasn't sure how serious he was being. The ironic smile fit with his abortion fanaticism about as much as the pierced ear did with his respectable appearance.

"She would've liked to see me thrown out of my own building. And every accidental power outage got pinned on me like it was a terrorist attack and then would appear instantly in the newspapers. These old buildings just have bad wiring. Do you have any idea what maintenance costs are for an old building like that?"

A few of the gamblers let out a loud communal groan, not out of sympathy with Knoll, though, but because one of the races had produced an unpopular result.

"And when she's not capable of looking after her own child, that gets pinned on me, too. Or the driver is guilty." Knoll signaled to the girl behind the counter that he'd like another cup of tea, since he'd gulped the first one down when it was still scalding hot. "What're you going to do now that you're out of a job and an apartment?"

Didn't miss a beat. And Brenner might have fallen for Knoll's concerned tone. Because the pro-life boss had years of practice, of course, coaxing a vulnerable person over to his side. But Brenner kept his cool and answered absolutely correctly, "At the moment, I'm not worried in the least."

"I've been searching for a bodyguard for the longest time."

"Aha."

"You could do the same job for me that you did for Kressdorf. As of immediately."

Brenner was speechless for a moment. He couldn't

believe how shamelessly Knoll was already scheming about how next to provoke the Frau Doctor.

"You wouldn't have to run around with a walkie-talkie and a revolver. It'd be enough for me if you worked as my driver."

Fortunately, at that moment Knoll's cell phone rang. Or unfortunately, I don't know which I should say. You never know when all is said and done: Was it more fortunate or was it more unfortunate? Will you regret it or not? Not to mention being born. A person's got to decide even the tiniest little thing in total blindness. The good lord's a bit of a sadist about it, because you never know: this or that, what's better for me and all involved when all is said and done? Brenner's the perfect example right now: would everything have turned out even worse if Knoll's cell phone hadn't rung and Brenner had given him the answer that was perched on the tip of his tongue, and what kind of answer would Knoll have given him in return? We can't know all that, or is it unfortunate that the phone call spared Brenner from answering, *summa summarum*, resulting in fewer deaths?

Now, surely you know the interesting phenomenon of cell phone contagion. I won't go so far as to say the most serious disease worldwide, but among the front-runners in any case. All it takes is the ring of one cell phone for everyone else to check whether they might have at least gotten a new message. That's exactly how it went for Brenner now. He played nervously with his phone as if he were silencing a call, while he listened to Knoll explain and calm down his callers, they shouldn't let the reports about the kidnapping dissuade them, because clear as day, the clinic itself is behind the kidnapping, and so the week's motto: rosary now more than ever.

After ten minutes of listening to Knoll talk on the phone, it got unbearable for him, and so he called someone, too. Believe it or not, Bank Director Reinhard. Without the job offer from Knoll, which Brenner had never taken seriously, he probably wouldn't have come up with the idea. Sure, Reinhard had always been friendly to Brenner, never arrogant, where you might think he's looking down at you. Once in Kitzbühel they chatted about hunting, and another time even about nature. Trees, birds, all of it. And one thing you can't forget: when Reinhard's chauffeur wasn't around, Kressdorf sometimes loaned Brenner out to him. Maybe that's a way of demonstrating friendship among the better people, just like how the little people might lend and borrow tools among themselves, salt, milk, an egg, and the middle people, maybe the car or the spouse, so among the better-off you'd say, *you know what, take my driver, I don't need him just now, he'll get you out to Klosterneuburg pronto.*

But don't go thinking it bothered Brenner. Because Reinhard—always a good tipper, don't even ask. Brenner hadn't told the bank director that he had no interest in hunting, of course, and now he was glad about that. Because otherwise, Reinhard certainly never would've said he was such a good driver that in case he ever stopped working for Kressdorf for some reason, he could be in touch anytime.

Brenner hadn't taken it seriously at the time, because first of all, he had no intention of swapping Helena for Reinhard anyway, and second of all, life experience told him that a guy like Bank Director Reinhard enjoys appearing as his

Sunday best, but when it comes down to it, there's a secretary saying, *we'll call you.*

What can I say, that's exactly how it was. With Reinhard's supposedly private number, Brenner advanced only as far as the secretary, and naturally, the Herr Director wasn't in, and in case the Herr Director should ever be truly in need of a driver, we'll call you. Brenner didn't need to go back out into the rain for this short conversation, but he didn't exactly want to make the call with Knoll on the phone next to him, and although it initially struck him as a good phone booth there beneath the covered entrance, the loud ventilation ended up sending him outside.

I have to be completely honest: no one who saw Brenner standing there in the rain would have guessed his detective past. Or predicted how in the coming weeks he would shake up the city. And you see, it's for these things exactly that I admire Brenner. Because he didn't give up after the faux-friendly "We'll call you." Instead he called up the Hotel Imperial and asked for Bank Director Reinhard.

You should know: once while they were waiting in Kitzbühel, Reinhard's driver had told Brenner that Reinhard kept a permanent suite at the Imperial where he liked to go on his lunch hour to stretch out a bit. Because, stressful sixteen-hour days, and how do you think he always manages to still make the drive to Klosterneuburg when he's tired from business lunches, or just wants to relax a little now and then? That's what he had the hotel suite for. But Reinhard never said "hotel room" or "suite," instead, listen closely: "refuge." And he always said that Churchill always said that "with a nap midday I get two days in one."

On this day, though, Director Reinhard must not have had time for two days, because Brenner didn't get hold of him at his refuge, either, and so he went back inside the betting parlor.

"Phone calls constantly!" Knoll said apologetically. Because he must not have noticed that in the meantime Brenner had made a phone call, too. "And? Have you thought it over?"

"What?"

"Are you going to work for me?"

"That would look great to the Frau Doctor," Brenner said helplessly, and gestured to the waitress for the bill.

"Enough already!" Knoll yelled, a bit frazzled, and turned his cell phone off in mid-ring. "You'll have to excuse me," he sighed, "but you can't imagine what kind of an uproar my people are in. They're being called kidnappers and murderers in broad daylight."

"At least they're getting a taste of their own medicine."

Brenner simply couldn't resist that one. But Knoll dismissed it as if it were nothing. "You're an ex-cop, you know the first thing that gets asked after a crime: who's profiting from it?"

"I'm wondering how you know that I used to be a cop."

Because, so it goes. Brenner was fairly certain at first that Knoll wasn't behind the kidnapping. And this attempt to breed suspicion made Brenner mistrustful all over again.

Knoll just looked at him sympathetically, though. "You wonder why I know something about your past, but you're confident that I would go and kidnap a child?"

"You threatened the Frau Doctor that you'd take her child away."

Knoll hesitated a moment, and then his seductive smile climbed from deep within him and stopped just before reaching his lips. "A threat made without any witnesses can be easily refuted. But I want to be frank with you. I think you're a good person. Truly, it happened in a moment of anger. I said something to Frau Doctor Kressdorf that one shouldn't say. But I said it differently. I didn't say anything about myself. I asked her whether she wasn't afraid that the good lord, from whom she'd taken so many children, might take her child away, too, some day."

"It's the same thing," Brenner protested.

At that moment, several of the screens hopped from snooker to dog racing.

"Good lord!" Knoll said once more. "Not to me. First of all, I'm no kidnapper, and second, I'm not stupid."

"And the good lord is stupid, or what?"

When they were suspended in slow motion, you could see how the muscular bodies of the dogs deformed out of sheer centrifugal force. Their flews were blown straight back and almost didn't catch up with their heads, their saliva flew with the bets into the sand, and Brenner wished that time would stand still in this lovely twilight created by the rainy day and the flat screens, because he had the feeling that there was no stopping now, and that everything had already been decided long before the first dog crossed the finish line.

"Listen to me: this kidnapping doesn't benefit me in any way."

"Unless the kidnappers don't make contact, and the Frau Doctor shuts down the clinic because it's her last hope for her child to turn up again."

By all appearances, Brenner spoke objectively. His eyes were glued to the screen and his words clung to his sense of reason. But the worm had worked its way in, he noticed it right away. Because the suspicion aroused by Knoll began to nag at him.

"We haven't gotten that far yet," Knoll said. "It used to look like we'd be the ones who'd shut down under public pressure and have to leave."

Brenner nodded in order to act like he was listening to Knoll. To his arguments. But he was only really listening to the worm that nagged at him.

"Up till now the kidnapping's only helped the clinic," Knoll blathered on. "Police protection round the clock. Public opinion wholeheartedly against us."

But while the dogs crawled breakneck around the bend and somersaulted over each other in slow motion, as if that in itself were the contest, Brenner could only think about what Knoll had said before. About the good lord. The good lord might have personally taken Helena. And a terrible fear took hold of Brenner that he might possibly have an almighty thug as an opponent.

"They just want to delay my terminating their lease. Until their new Super Practice in MegaLand is finished," Knoll said.

"Why MegaLand?" Like a track-standing cyclist trying to maintain his balance, who, at the last moment before falling over, rescues himself with the push of a pedal, Brenner rescued himself back into the conversation again. "It's going to be a recreational park. Golf course, swimming pool, shops, movie theater, that kind of thing."

"Haven't you ever noticed how private practices are

popping up in retail centers these days? The dental clinic in the train station, the cosmetic surgeon at the mall."

"Sure, I've noticed the dental clinic."

"And an abortion between shopping and bowling at MegaLand, it all fits smartly together. *Baby Be Gone* in designer ambience. With a ten-percent-off coupon for the next time."

Brenner was almost relieved to see Knoll's eyes light up with zeal now. Suddenly, he was back on familiar turf with the pro-life boss. Unbelievable, though, how easily a fanatic like that can rattle you when you're feeling weak and running around with an enormous amount of guilt.

"*Baby Be Gone*. You're pretty cynical."

"I'm not cynical. The people responsible for such a thing are cynical. Mega-Abortion-Land, financed by a million children's deaths."

"Alright, that's enough." Things were slowly turning sour for Brenner.

"Something like this has to be professionally branded so that it sells. Mega-Abortion-Land," Knoll said with that amused look again. "Maybe I should go into business with them and sell them the name." He was getting carried away by vanity now, and Brenner hoped he might make a decisive slip. "At her new super clinic in MegaLand she'll have to triple her earnings in order to recoup the costs. But I don't want to bother you with our fanaticism."

Knoll pronounced "fanaticism" as if he'd had some kind of tainted alphabet soup for breakfast that only had quotation marks in it, which were gurgling up inside him at this very moment. "Or might I still convince an old workhorse like you of the miracle of life?"

"I've even looked at the brochures that your people hand out in front of the clinic. Nature sure puts on a show."

"A show!" Knoll repeated, scornfully.

Brenner had drawn out the word "show" in order to provoke Knoll. "Miracle" would have worked, too, because back when the brochure fell into his hands, he'd thought to himself: *hats off to nature*. It wasn't new to him, of course, what happens behind the scenes during those nine months, but a while indeed since he'd first applied himself to the subject back home in Puntigam, and at that time, of course, he'd only been interested in the procreative part, or better yet, on preventing new life.

"It's only at a certain age that you can fully appreciate nature," Brenner formulated, a compromise, as it were. "It's true, though: your fanatic views do nothing for me. I saw too many fully grown deaths when I was on the force—you can't be looking out for a bunch of cells, too."

"So when does life begin for you, if I may ask?"

Brenner wanted to steer the conversation gradually in another direction, but he had to give Knoll a quick answer. "Where I'm from, in Puntigam—"

"You're from Puntigam? Where the beer's from?"

You see, that really got Knoll smiling, he was happy to actually meet someone from Puntigam.

"Exactly. In Puntigam, there was an old saying that children were told. *Before you were born, you were just flying around with the gnats.*"

"I know that one, too. You were just flying around with the gnats. We used to say that as children, too."

"That's a good enough explanation for me," Brenner said. "That you fly with the gnats before—and maybe you fly with the gnats again afterward, too. I think it's a good solution. For logistical reasons alone. That's why I don't understand why you'd waste this short stopover arguing about life. When you consider how short the time is compared to the gnats' time."

"You have that worked out quite comfortably. And otherwise, there's nothing else that interests you about life?"

"I'm interested in what you want from me."

"I want you to find the girl for me."

The gamblers grew restless, and Brenner, too, couldn't tear his gaze away from the screen, as the news came that one of the two dogs, whose sudden collapse was being shown over and over again, had broken its neck. Which is why he thought Knoll was talking about Helena at first, until he noticed the photo Knoll had laid on the table.

"How old would you guess this girl is?"

"No idea," Brenner said, giving the photo a quick once-over. "Sixteen? Fifteen?"

It wasn't a particularly good photo. A girl with long dark hair, walking, photographed from an odd angle, like an actress being hunted by the paparazzi. And only on the second glance did Brenner recognize the surroundings, because the photo had been taken right in front of the entrance to the abortion clinic.

"Twelve."

"Huh, crazy, the Mediterraneans often look downright grown-up for their age. A pretty girl," Brenner said, indifferently, as if Knoll had shown him a photo of his favorite niece.

"Twelve," Knoll repeated, and all the more somber for it. "On her way to the abortion clinic."

"Is that illegal?"

"No, it's not." Knoll reminded Brenner of an oracle who says everything twice, first normally, then a second time with grave foreboding, listen: "No, it's not. For the unborn, there is no protection in our society."

He pushed the photo at Brenner and offered him 10,000 euros if he found the girl, whose name he didn't know.

"Seems to me, the unborn matter more to you guys than the born do," Brenner said. "I was on the force for nineteen years. And I didn't go trumpeting all over the place that I was fighting for the lives of the born, either."

Knoll didn't let himself be provoked, though. You could tell right away that he was used to these kinds of discussions, and he had roped Brenner into a conversation about unborn life and about morality at large, for and against, pro and contra—you could transcribe it for the pages of *Religion Today* every single time.

And to be perfectly honest: if Brenner didn't have his own brand of fanaticism, in which he believed himself to be the only one capable of finding Helena, and if rage wasn't burning in him like a vaccine, then I wouldn't exactly stick my hand in the fire about whether Knoll stood a chance at persuading him yet. And maybe Brenner would be standing in front of the abortion clinic today with a rosary and an embryo sign and a pious expression on his face, and on the other side of the clinic's entrance, the young security woman with the lawn-mowed do would have no idea that the old nut was actually Brenner, who used to be a cop and a detective and everything.

And that would be the same Brenner who people tell heroic tales about today, the stuff of wonder, beginning with the cell phone that he swiped from Knoll's pocket in the betting parlor, allegedly like a real trickster thief. Seldom did anything in life go that smoothly for Brenner. You should know, Knoll made exactly the same mistake that Brenner did at the gas station and went to the bathroom at the betting parlor without his cell phone. And maybe Brenner only really took it because of that, in order to even the score for his own disgrace. But that's how people are, and if a person's solved the most spectacular murder case, then he's absolutely got to be a magician with the little things, too.

But, right now, something much more important. Because believe it or not, Bank Director Reinhard was calling Brenner back.

CHAPTER 9

Now why is Brenner back at the gas station? Are his pangs of guilt pulling him there? Does he want to take another look at the surveillance video? Or is he hoping that the gas station's drunks will adopt him, i.e., third musketeer?

Pay attention. Brenner was thinking to himself, *Milan will definitely know someone who can unlock Knoll's phone for me, the sort of thing someone at a gas station knows.* But no luck on that front, because instead of Milan there was another attendant behind the cash register. The two drunks were there, of course—should I say "again" or "still," I don't know, they might have lived there. In any case, they shot him a smirk but didn't say a word.

Brenner asked the new guy about Milan. The guy didn't want to say anything at first, but then he came out with it. Milan got fired. Picture this: he'd been keeping a case of beer up at the counter and selling it on the sly. And the whole thing got exposed in the police raid because the cops turned everything over and scrutinized it three times, of course, and what did they find? Just Milan's backdoor beer. In other words, Milan: second Brenner-victim of the day.

The new attendant just looked irritated by the question of whether he could unlock a cell phone because after the incident with his predecessor, he thought the company had sent a hired goon into the shop to test him. Nevertheless, he sold the test-goon a nonalcoholic beer, was even particularly friendly about it. Brenner stationed himself right back at the counter and briefly contemplated whether the answer might lie in Milan's dismissal. Maybe the case of beer was just a front and was actually a connection to the kidnapping because the attendant had seen something, and now was being made to keep his mouth shut due to the intrigue surrounding the case of beer.

Brenner was so captivated by this theory that he ordered an espresso and a second nonalcoholic beer.

So you see, contemplating nonsense: often very useful. Because without the contemplating he wouldn't have stayed as long as he did at the gas station. And then he wouldn't have been standing there with his second nonalcoholic beer when the woman from the surveillance video came in. He recognized her right away from her curls, which were so fiery red that, in all fairness, they had no business being at a gas station. She got a newspaper and a carton of milk, and asked for a pack of Marlboro Lights at the cash register. Interesting, though. She didn't stress the "a" in "Marlboro," but the middle instead, like this: "Marl*boo*ro." Brenner tried to make eye contact with the witness, but paying and pocketing the change and turning around and traipsing out were a single fluid movement with her, as if she were still being fast-forwarded on the video, and she walked past Brenner without even noticing him.

"South Tyrol!" Brenner yelled out, when she was closer to the exit than the cash register. Or actually, it was more of a murmur—no, too loud for a murmur, but too quiet for a yell, more of a medium middling volume. From the moment she asked for a pack of Marl*boo*ros, he'd been coming up with ways to take his guess that she was South Tyrolean and turn it into a line. But unfortunately, the new gas station attendant was incredibly nimble. He gave her back her change so fast, and she'd put it away so fast, that Brenner didn't have enough time to develop a good line.

As the woman walked past the drunks, with the milk and newspaper in one hand and the pack of Marl*boo*ros in the other, Brenner got morose. *My God*, he cursed to himself, silently, *I used to be able to come up with a line in a tenth of a second, I didn't even have to think about it. And now I have this trump in my hand, I can identify where she's from based on her cigarette pronunciation, and can you believe what I come up with?*

He knew from experience that in a situation like this you simply have to lean as far out the window as possible, put yourself in a dangerous situation, and then a good line will come swimming in on the adrenaline. Which is why—as the woman flew past the potato chip rack in the direction of the newspaper rack, and then past the newspaper rack in the direction of the impulse-item rack, and past the impulse-item rack in the direction of the door—he called out to her in a way that sounded like he was murmuring, but was indeed clear and unmistakably audible: "South Tyrol!"

And the line shall follow. That was the calculation, with the meal comes the appetite, it's the conversation that brings people together, stick your nose in other people's business and an irresistible line will follow. Calculated error, as it were. Because no line, near or far. The two-word line echoed through the gas station, enough to make Brenner sick. South Tyrol! Nothing embarrassing had happened to him in a while. Before, he would have at least said as she walked by: "Do they believe in love at first sight in South Tyrol—or were you planning to walk by a second time?" Or a thousand possibilities. But now, either on account of the pills or the nonalcoholic beer or quite simply from age, or a rusty brain, or withering hormones—in all events, no line.

Now, I don't know whether you know that the South Tyroleans are the most beautiful women in the world. Well, I've never been to Australia, but otherwise I can personally vouch that worldwide the South Tyroleans come in first, and then there's nothing for a while, because genetically it might just be the ideal mating: half Italian meets half Geierwally. Just so you understand what kind of pressure Brenner was under.

"That was a long time ago," the back of the South Tyrolean said. But turn around, not a chance. She stamped on toward the exit, without missing a step, because that was the Italian half that fueled the arrogant stamping.

"Could I have a Marl*boo*ro?" Brenner yelled out fast, just as the automatic doors were opening before her.

And believe it or not, she turned around and walked right up to Brenner. "You have good ears," she said, tearing open the pack and holding it out to him.

"It was the Marl*boo*ro," Brenner explained proudly, as he waved a dismissive hand at the pack of cigarettes. "Since I don't drink anymore, I don't smoke anymore either." And he pointed to the nonalcoholic label because he wanted to make himself a little interesting.

The South Tyrolean immediately took it upon herself to perform that twin feminine task, i.e., simultaneously rolling her eyes and twisting her mouth, arrogantly and in opposite directions.

Now before she turned away entirely, Brenner quickly added, "I need to ask you something important."

And then, of course, whether she'd seen anything thirty-three hours earlier.

It really just wasn't his day, though. Or the gas station just wasn't his place, maybe something wasn't right with the water. Because the woman was completely clueless. She didn't even know what he was referring to.

"But surely you saw something on TV or in the newspaper about—"

"I don't read the paper."

When a thing like that gets said by somebody who's just bought a newspaper, naturally you have to say: suspicious. There she was, standing in front of him with a carton of milk, a pack of Marl*boo*ros, and a newspaper, and explaining in her South Tyrolean accent: "The newspaper's too depresshing for me."

"So you just bought it because—"

My god, before he would have said, because of the love horoscope, because of the personal ads, anything, it doesn't even matter, just some slight suggestion—not too much subtext, well, okay, just a little—because these days if you make a woman laugh, you're already on the right path in the direction of, let's say, philosophical conversations.

"—because of the TV lishtings," the South Tyrolean claimed in her South Tyrolean accent. "Because the TV lishtings are always in the Friday paper. The news I throw away the minute I get home."

"And you don't watch TV, either," Brenner said. "You just read the listings."

You can see how he was already getting back into the swing a bit. Nothing compared to the old days, of course. Long gone are the days when he would have lay in wait for her by the recycling bins in front of her house—full throttle, as it were. Although, to be honest, he'd often idealized his past a little. Because in truth Brenner had never been full throttle—actually in reverse most of the time, or hand brake, broken starter, distributor out, wet spark plugs, that kind of thing. An irony of fate: Brenner owed his broad shoulders—which, in the eyes of women, lent him an energetic aura—to the endless push-starting of the stalled jalopy that was his life.

"Why wouldn't I watch TV?" the South Tyrolean replied. Because she might have come up with something better, too, but I always say, milk drinkers for the most part aren't that primed to return a stupid remark from a man with an even stupider remark. No, to be perfectly objective, like a South Tyrolean mountain peak asking itself, *why wouldn't I peer down into the valley below?*, she asked why she wouldn't watch TV.

"Then you must have seen something on TV about the kidnapping that happened right in front of your house."

"*Ma Dai*, you're not too shwift, are you," she sighed. "That was a joke! The newspapers have been calling nonshtop since yeshterday, the police have been here twice, I can't take one shtep without someone asking whether I saw anything! Jusht because yeshterday I accidentally happened to walk to the right of the gas pump instead of the left like I normally do after I shop."

"Obviously suspicious."

"Exactly. You know, it's because that big clunker was shtanding in my way when I went to throw my empty bottles away. And because of that I show up on the damn shurveillance video."

"So?"

"I'm going to tell you a secret. Even if you end up needing a pshychiatrisht because of it. Do you want to hear it?"

"I think I'll manage."

"I don't like cars. I didn't even see your fancy sleigh ride, even though you parked it so wide it was blocking my way. It wasn't till the video that I saw that heap of yours. Even though I practically had to walk a kilometer around it. Otherwise, I never would have gone up there."

"Up? Up where?" Brenner asked. "Everything's flat at a gas station."

"Up on the video."

Brenner was awfully glad that she didn't get the joke either. "It's not my car. I'm just the chauffeur."

The South Tyrolean looked at him as if that was no excuse, but then she said, "Oh yeah, that's what they said on TV. You should have kept a closer eye on the kid."

"And you didn't see anything? No one leaving with a child?"

"You know, you're actually the firsht to ask me that queshtion."

"Alright already," Brenner said under his breath.

But that must have been exactly what she was looking

for, because now that Brenner had given up, she said: "You're the only one of the whole idiotic slew who I'd like to help. There's shomething about you I like. With your shtrange eyes. And your shirt's untucked."

Brenner tucked in his shirt, and the two drunks grinned stupidly. Their eyes were glazed from staring, and their heads were craned so far from eavesdropping that their ears were practically brushing against the ad for motor oil that was hanging from the ceiling.

"But I'm more the kind of person who keeps to hershelf," the woman said. "I even have to take pills for depresshion."

"And do they do anything?"

"Of course. If they didn't, do you think I'd be capable of crossing the shtreet? But you know what I think's a sham? I wouldn't expect regular shoppers to wind up on security cameras here. I'm not saying anything about them monitoring the drivers—in case one takes off without paying, you have his lischense plate. That I can undershtand. An ordinary shopper, though, who only buys milk, doesn't need to be taped doing it."

"It happens automatically," Brenner said. "If they're taping the drivers and a shopper runs into the frame, then they're automatically on it."

"So now it's shupposed to be my fault," the South Tyrolean protested. And then she smiled because Brenner looked so dejected. "Don't worry so much, the little one will turn up again. I can feel it. You can trusht me completely on that, I have a feeling for this sort of thing. The girl's fine. Besides, the contractor has plenty of dough. It can't be true that the kidnappers haven't made contact."

"On the one hand, you have a feeling; on the other hand, you make a logical argument."

"And you? Only drinking nonalcoholic beer?"

Then she left.

That was something! Just said it and left. As the automatic doors opened for her, something new occurred to Brenner.

"South Tyrolean!" he yelled. This time with a note of urgency. To no avail, though. She didn't turn around, and when he yelled his cell phone number out after her, she was already through the door and outside before he got to the last digit. He watched through the glass how she walked left around the gas pump, *good figure and everything*, Brenner thought to himself, *if I had met her in my day*, and he kept gazing after her as she crossed the street, with the newspaper and milk in her left hand and the pack of Marl*boo*ros in her right, and disappeared into the house opposite the gas station.

CHAPTER 10

He didn't get the cell phone unlocked at the gas station, and he didn't find anything out from the South Tyrolean, either. But pay attention to what I'm telling you: nothing's ever for nothing in life, most of the time you find something different than what you're looking for. And Brenner now found someone returning a rental car to the gas station. A purple Ford Mondeo, and ten minutes later it was his Mondeo because he told them they didn't need to wash it, and so you see, he drove the Mondeo to the Lilliput Café, and there they unlocked the cell phone for him right away.

PATRON OF LILLIPUT CAFÉ. Naturally, that's how it was later portrayed in the newspaper, as if Brenner had been a regular there, those people really busted his chops on that one, don't even ask. But my feelings vis-à-vis the Lilliput Café are very clear. Listen up: if after everything that's happened, someone's still pointing a finger at the Lilliput Café, then I honestly have to say, it's roughly like telling a starving person to put the menu down just because, according to Chinese thought, the micronutrients aren't in the fifth house right now.

Brenner knew the Lilliput Café because at least once a week he'd picked Kressdorf up from the construction site near there. Or better put, from the planned construction site, on account of the protests of course, and there being not much to see except construction fences and steam shovels and pits. Or he would bring Helena by so that Kressdorf could spend a few minutes with his daughter between appointments. They'd ride the Lilliput train through the wooded areas of the Prater Park and around the site slated for MegaLand, and so Brenner would sometimes wait for the two of them at the Lilliput Café.

Helena was a total fanatic for the Lilliput train rides, and Brenner was a little jealous of her father, because if just once he'd said to his daughter, *you know what, today Herr Simon's going to take you for a ride on the train*, he would have done it on the spot, no discussion. But no, when the ride was over Helena would always bawl her head off, and do you think Kressdorf might have given in just once? He didn't let his daughter wear him down, though. No, Herr Papa got even stricter and: "That's enough now."

Just so you understand why Brenner was so familiar with the Lilliput Café. Because he never went for the other things that were there, smuggled cigarettes or a fake wristwatch, and the Lilliput Café's main business was with the parents, of course. Driven to despair by the screams of their Lilliput-train-addicted children, they could get their mothers' little helpers at the Lilliput Café, more convenient than the pharmacy and qualitatively better, more effective and all, where you find yourself saying, *it may not be entirely legal but at least I can make it another three days smiling at my child instead of tossing him headfirst over the fence so that the neighbors can smile at him.*

They unlocked the cell phone for him in a matter of seconds. His nonalcoholic beer wasn't even in front of him yet before he was holding the phone in his hand with a new PIN. You're going to say, Brenner must have deliberated over the PIN for a long time, because what's the best combination of numbers to choose? But quite the opposite, Brenner shot it out like a pistol: 1706, because that was Helena's birthday. But then he reconsidered after all, because a gravestone suddenly floated in front of his eyes, where the date of birth always appears above the date of death, bad omen, as it were. To be on the safe side, he went with a date of death instead. You should know that on November 12, 2008, the last member of Jimi Hendrix's band, Mitch Mitchell, died—because none of them was granted a long life. Jimi Hendrix was born in November, Mitch Mitchell died in November, and believe it or not, Noel Redding also had an 11 on his gravestone because he died on the eleventh of May. But Brenner was already using Noel Redding for his own cell phone's PIN, so he dedicated the PIN on Knoll's cell phone to Mitch Mitchell, i.e. 1211. So you weren't totally wrong, he did mull the PIN over a bit.

But he didn't get around to listening to Knoll's voicemail, because: "Hey, Herr Simon, over here!"

Just what he needed. But that's exactly how it goes when you seek out familiar places. You have to take into account that you might run into people you know. At least it wasn't Kressdorf himself, but just the watchdog from his construction site. Brenner didn't recognize him right away because beefcakes with crewcuts and tattoos up to their eardrums, you see them so often on the street today that you can't know them all by heart. It was the white straw he was sucking on that gave him away, i.e., nicotine withdrawal. Also the befreckled foreman who he came in with. You should know, the few times Brenner had seen the nicotine-addicted watchdog, he'd always been with the foreman from the MegaLand site, as if he always needed to be hanging on to one of them, cigarette or foreman, didn't matter which.

"Waiting on a new job offer?" the foreman asked, and a hundred thousand freckles loomed in front of Brenner's face.

"With your qualifications, it's no wonder your phone's ringing up a storm!" the watchdog continued and pointed at Knoll's phone with his plastic straw. Because now that it was unlocked, the messages were chiming up a lightning storm like you wouldn't believe.

"A nice steady ball like you two are rolling is what I'm looking for," Brenner answered. "Sitting in a café all day on Kressdorf's dime, that's for me."

"You wouldn't be very happy working with us. There's nothing left at KREBA for someone like you who goes around losing people's kids."

Brenner was getting annoyed by the belt of freckles around the foreman's stupid grin, because something as nice as a face full of freckles can make a cruel smile even crueler. I can understand where Brenner was coming from—strictly speaking, it's a betrayal of freckles.

"Because Kressdorf doesn't have any more kids to lose," the one with the straw explained.

"Explaining somebody else's joke," Brenner said, "is that a side effect when you quit smoking?"

The nicotine addict sucked on his straw like a wheezing asthmatic on an inhaler. And it might have done him some good, because once he got his fill again, all of a sudden he acted completely normal with Brenner. Even professional, presenting himself as a colleague, because construction-site security, i.e., armed security services: practically the police.

Brenner asked him how he knew for a fact that he used to be on the police force, but please—it was a convenient topic for him. So he let the straw-man pass, and he acted like it was the highest caliber of police work, spending all day on the lookout so that nobody steals from the construction site or damages the fences or goes sniffing around the site or hangs up a banner against the Prater Park development. And I honestly have to say, with a project like MegaLand, where you've got half the city against you because your boss only has enough money to bribe the other half, it's not completely outrageous for the security guard to puff up his feathers a little.

Brenner let the two of them explain the world to him for a while, what Kressdorf does all wrong, what Congressman Stachl does all wrong, what all of them at the top do all wrong, and how someone just needs to do a better job of explaining to the masses that there's something in it for them, too, if the Prater starts charging an entrance fee, because golf, tennis, wellness, movies, shopping, entertainment squared instead of just trees and pampas—for that even the little guy doesn't mind paying a little. Brenner let them pump him about the kidnapping, i.e., where exactly, when exactly, how exactly. And he was even obliging enough to laugh at the crass jokes they cracked about Knoll. When you're a detective, you can't be fussy about things like this—you don't get anything out of people if you don't let them talk.

So what did he learn? Listen up, Knoll's alarm system

company had installed cameras not only in the building's lobby, and in the elevator, and in the stairwells, and filmed everyone who entered the building—the police also found two cameras that Knoll had mounted around the time of the first water main break.

Brenner explained that there's nothing more perverse than an abortion clinic with surveillance cameras, and the two of them agreed with him one hundred percent. But while the watchdog repeated for the third time that there was nothing more perverse, something more perverse occurred to him as he was talking. He presented his idea of what was more perverse as though it were proof that there was nothing more perverse. My god, he had other qualities besides an inflated ego. He and the foreman were so engrossed in conversation now that it was operating like talk among old friends. And that was the best thing that could have happened for Brenner. Because they didn't notice that Brenner had been waiting the whole time for just the right moment.

You should know, there's a right moment for everything. For plants, when to plant them, when to water them, when to harvest them; for animals, when to feed them, when to milk them, when to slaughter them; for children, when to make them, when to nurse them, when to kick them out on their own; for fingernails, when to cut them, when to file them, when to polish them; and hair, too, very important. But only a very few know how important the right moment is for the detective counterquestion.

"What do you two have to say about her?" Brenner placed the photo that Knoll had given him on the table.

"Jailbait," they said almost in unison—a well-rehearsed

team. But they were of no help to Brenner because they didn't recognize the girl. The security guard just got excited at the prospect of proving his professionalism to Brenner. Because he immediately pulled out his cell phone and took a photo of the photo. "In case I come across her, I'll let you know."

"But only after you come on top of her," the foreman said with a smirk, and Brenner wondered whether it was his smirk that was crooked or if it only came off that way because his freckles were so unevenly distributed.

"Of course," the nicotine-nursling said, bringing up the rear of the joke again. "Only after I've come on top of her."

But then his freckled smirk got even more crooked, so crooked that it was like they'd passed the nicotine pipe around and the substance in the pipe was distorting Brenner's vision. His vision wasn't the problem, though, because Brenner: A-plus vision. If this weren't the case, then when he finally turned around and followed the freckled asshole's glance, he wouldn't have seen as clearly as he did what was playing out in front of the Lilliput Café's only window.

"Thanks for the warning," he called out to the two of them from the bathroom, while outside, Kressdorf and Congressman Stachl were climbing out of Kressdorf's jeep, which was parked right next to his Mondeo. The joke was on him, that much is obvious, because the two of them knew the whole time that they were waiting there for their boss.

No way out now except through the bathroom window. Then Brenner walked along the Hauptallee a bit and listened to Knoll's voicemail, because he didn't dare make his way back to the Mondeo until Kressdorf was gone.

My dear swan, Brenner hadn't been in a funk like this

in a long time. And the fact that the idiot watchdog and his Pippi Longstocking had let him fall right into it could only bear half the blame for why his mood just soured with every step. Above all there was the crap that Knoll Jr. was whining about to Knoll's voicemail. Because that was a burden that would have merited half a year's psychological counseling right off the bat for any civil servant—and from the most attractive police psychologist no less.

Brenner wasn't an impatient man otherwise, but he was on the search for a kidnapped child, and with something like this you've got to hurry. You can't just listen to voicemails until the kidnapped victim is old enough to say, *I choose of my own free will to remain with my kidnapper because I've gotten used to him*. No, you've got to be swift. Neverending voicemail messages are hard enough to endure in normal life, but in Brenner's situation it could be filed, strictly speaking, under "accomplice to murder." His ear practically fell asleep listening, and although on principle he was one to always hold the phone to his left ear, he actually switched briefly to his right. He wondered whether Knoll ever listened to these messages at all. Or maybe it was just a personal hotline where he let the church ladies talk. For those times when it's necessary to request of an excessive talker: *speak your interesting thoughts into a plastic bag, then place the bag before my door, I'll listen to them later*.

But as Brenner was about to turn the phone back off, a message came in that interested him. And I don't mean the message where Knoll called and offered the honest finder a finder's fee of a hundred euros for bringing his lost cell phone to his office, because that one came right at the start.

No, pay attention: a man's gravelly voice said to the inbox, "Saturday, nine a.m. One million and no further negotiations."

Thirty-five hours after Helena disappeared from her Zone of vehicular Transparency, and five hours after Brenner got sent out into the rain by the police, and four hours after Knoll stressed that it wasn't him but rather the good lord who might have called Helena back to him, Brenner became aware that he still had an irrational fear in his bones of the good lord. Now how did he become aware of this? Believe it or not, for one second, or maybe just for a hundredth of a second—a thousandth of a second if you ask me—the gravelly voice sent by the satellite to the voicemail really did sound like a voice from beyond. Just listen: "Nine a.m. One million and no further negotiations."

And the voice named a Schrebergarten that Brenner didn't know. But an old woman who was out strolling explained to him that he had to go back the other way because Greenland, the colony of garden plots in question, was on the other side of the Lilliput Café, just a little ways from where the Lilliput train loops around. Absolutely correct information, and then he found *Greenland* on a park map, too. Pay attention, if you're coming from the Lilliput train, the colony is situated right behind Happel Stadium, or if you're coming from the underage prostitutes along the Baby Strip, it's behind the velodrome. Best you take note of the address right now, because that's where Brenner was going next: the Greenland Schrebergarten in Prater Park, second gate, first row, third plot on the left.

CHAPTER 11

Schrebergartens are a topic all their own, of course. Much has been said about them because it's widely accepted that their trees and shrubs grow so well on account of a corpse being the best fertilizer. I don't count myself among the people who say, *more dead bodies in Schrebergartens than in cemeteries*, but the particular burden of waste is greater in any case. Because at normal cemeteries they take the worst stuff out of the deceased, the batteries from their pacemakers, the artificial joints, the dentures, and the silicone parts, so that the groundwater doesn't suffer too much. But Schrebergarten corpses are mostly buried hush-hush and in a hurry, batteries and all. Oddly enough, the plants don't seem to mind—they thrive like blazes—but long term, the groundwater's got to be paying for it.

It took Brenner roughly half an hour to find the right gate, but only half a minute to get into the cottage.

That he got in so easily wasn't necessarily a bad sign yet, in case you're thinking *if the Schrebergarten cottage is this poorly secured, then no kidnapping victim's going to be found here.* I could tell you about one case after another where kidnapping victims were held in completely normal houses—no waterfalls, no spring gun, no anything. And no discussion anyway with a two-year-old child. There doesn't have to be any high-security apparatus, because the only important thing's that nobody comes up with the idea to look there.

Brenner was cautious of course, because when you're a stranger in a Schrebergarten, you always fear for your life, no need to throw a kidnapping into the bargain. But not cautious in the sense that he would've wound himself around the doorframe with a Glock in both hands or danced a wide arc around a booby trap like he was at the world tango championship. First of all, he didn't have a gun on him anyway, and besides, in a situation like this you only make everything worse by having a gun, because without a gun, worst case, you can always talk your way out of it somehow should you run right into the kidnapper's arms.

Unfortunately, though, neither kidnapper nor Helena in the living room. Just a completely deserted living room. Never in his life did an abode appear quite so godforsaken. And it could have been stated without exaggeration that this godforsaken weekend hell depressed Brenner to death—if he wasn't already in such a mood that it would've been a huge improvement for something to depress him to death.

And the kitchen, too, godforsaken. And the bathroom, godforsaken. And upstairs in the tiny attic, godforsaken. And that little bit of a cellar, also godforsaken. The word "godforsaken" engraved itself methodically into Brenner's brain. You can see how the worm was nagging at him again—this time with the fear that it could be the good lord himself who was leaving him there to wallow until nine the next morning.

He set up camp in the tiny attic bedroom and looked through the blinds at the walkway below. There were still twelve hours until the handover at nine o'clock. Or better put, three hours. Not what you're thinking, though, that the handover got moved up. No, Brenner was so utterly exhausted after this dreadful day and the sleepless night at the police station and the conversation with Knoll and the encounter with the South Tyrolean and the escape from the Lilliput Café and the trip out to Klosterneuburg, that he fell asleep thinking that he would in no way fall asleep here.

Now, what had he been looking for in Klosterneuburg tonight? You should know, when Bank Director Reinhard called Brenner that afternoon, he was calling about an appointment in Klosterneuburg, saying, "Would you fancy paying me a visit at eight o'clock in my domicile?"

Because "domicile" and "refuge," that's the kind of language Reinhard used, but the padded expressions suited his big persona. Besides the central bank and two or three restaurants, his domicile in Klosterneuburg and his refuge at the Imperial were the most important addresses for his driver. He slept nights at the domicile and days at the refuge. Because these days, when you lead an enterprise of 10,000 employees, you have to get every last drop out of your leisure time; otherwise you might as well pack it in.

At first Brenner was even glad to have something else to do that evening, because thirteen hours in a Schrebergarten cottage waiting for money to change hands isn't that interesting. But then, as he was standing in front of the domicile with Reinhard, he asked himself what it was that he was looking for there. Reinhard acted as if the conversation had never been about the prospect of becoming his driver. He was only interested in having Brenner telling him in minute detail again about the kidnapping at the gas station.

He took Brenner to a pleasant little place in the garden and ordered drinks from the house by phone. And believe it or not, Congressman Stachl brought the drinks out. Because with tabloids and scandals everybody's the same, the nobodies and the somebodies, they all want to know as firsthand as possible exactly what it was like. At least Reinhard let Brenner tell his story in peace, whereas the Congressman kept interrupting him. He wanted to understand very thoroughly. But his questions didn't get him anywhere. Because naturally Brenner didn't mention anything about Knoll or the planned handover in the Schrebergarten cottage. Congressman Stachl could have been a little friendlier instead of just glowering out from beneath his bushy eyebrows, as if nothing surrounding his city development project had happened in a long time that was as troublesome to him as this kidnapping.

Brenner sat there telling them exactly what they already knew until they got bored. Then the bank director accompanied him back to his Mondeo and gave him an encouraging pat on the shoulder in farewell, i.e., *things will look up again*. And at the last second he reached into his jacket pocket and pressed an envelope into Brenner's hand. "Perhaps this will be of some help to you."

Brenner was still holding the envelope in his hand when he woke up in the Schrebergarten attic. Counting the envelope containing his last month's pay that Natalie had brought him, this now made the second envelope of money in one day, and slowly it began to seem to Brenner that he really was the kidnapper, getting paid the ransom in installments.

Interesting, though: he not only still had the envelope in his hand upon waking up, but also the thought still in his mind that he could in no way fall asleep here. And this thought is the best proof of how the wakeful mind often doesn't do its best thinking. Because, *don't fall asleep here*, any bloody layman could have given him this advice—pivotal mistake, as it were—never fall asleep at the scene of the handover, where the gangster might show up early and kill you. But one thing you can't forget: Brenner's greatest strength was exactly that. The detective half-sleep. Because he wasn't sleeping deeply of course, just half-sleeping. And with the other half he watched over the house and over himself, sleeping.

Now, you should know, the best thoughts of Brenner's life always came to him while he was half asleep. It's a great misconception that people have—the more awake, the more concentrated, the more rested, the better for their heads. Because just like a light that's too bright can be bad for the eyes, so, too, can a mind that's too awake be not at all good for the thoughts. And in truth a half-asleep person can always outmatch an awake person by a long shot, no discussion. Far too many thoughts get in the way of thinking with an awake person, but the good lord whispers directly into the mind of the sleeping person. Only you can't fall asleep completely, or else you might not hear him.

Watch closely: while he was half asleep it occurred to Brenner that he had overlooked one little thing amid the onslaught of voicemails. Because place and time for the hand over of money had been made known to Knoll one day before the kidnapping!

So when shortly before nine an old man opened the garden gate, Brenner had been wide awake for a while. The old man didn't have Helena with him, and he didn't come off as a kidnapper, either, but nonetheless—to be feared. Because the typical Schrebergarten pensioner, without any kidnapping or murder thrown in, already fills the bill more than amply, i.e., overweight, limping, lawn-mowing, fence-painting, grilling, TV-watching, politicizing, groaning, weeding, car-washing, undershirt-wearing, opinion-expressing, hard-of-hearing crankiness personified.

But let's not be unfair. Because the old man being hard of hearing, that alone was an enormous advantage for Brenner. Hard of hearing an advantage, and the heavy breathing an advantage, too. Because once he'd shuffled into the living room, the heavy breathing prevented the Schrebergartener from making any effort to go up to the attic. And his being hard of hearing resulted in Brenner being able to understand nearly every word from the attic when Knoll arrived at nine sharp with a briefcase of money and a stooge in tow.

"One million?" the hard-of-hearing pensioner barked.

"Go ahead and count it," Knoll answered at a normal indoor volume, but Brenner understood him anyway because when someone says what you're expecting him to say, then you understand him easier, even from a distance.

"What did you say?" the retiree asked, because he couldn't understand Knoll even at close range. Possible that this rule about easier comprehension of what's expected only applies to "from a distance" and not to "hard of hearing while at close range."

"Go ahead and count it," Knoll said as softly as he had

before because that was his volume, he didn't let the rules of the game get dictated by someone else, no, always nudging the others a little to where he wanted them.

The stooge said nothing because—silent stooge.

"One thousand, two thousand, three thousand," the Schrebergartener began, and Brenner thought to himself, *if he's going to count to a million, I'm going back to sleep*.

"Seventy-two thousand," the Schrebergarten boss said, and then stopped. "And where are the six hundred and seventy-two euros?"

Knoll either said nothing or said "Kiss my ass" so quietly that neither Brenner nor the pensioner heard it.

"I still do business in schillings, I don't do euros," the old man bellowed. "And one million is still seventy-two thousand six hundred and seventy-two euros and not seventy-two thousand euros flat."

"As long as you're not front-ending me in old francs," Knoll said, dry as dust, and in the tension of the moment Brenner had to be careful not to let out a laugh.

"Exact calculation, my friend," the old dogmatist wheezed.

"If you were being so exact about everything," Knoll said, and a few other words, too, that Brenner couldn't make out, but Knoll's bad mood he understood nevertheless.

"If I were going to be exact, it would come to seventy-two thousand six hundred and seventy-four euros and forty cents. Actually, forty-two cents, but the two you can have, and the forty I'll give you, too. But six hundred seventy-two euros, that's still nine thousand schillings, roughly calculated. To be exact . . ."

What was happening now Brenner couldn't see from

where he was, but I'll put it this way: it took exactly as long as you'd need to pull an antediluvian pocket calculator out of your blue work pants and to type in 672 × 13.76.

"...it comes to nine thousand two hundred and forty-six schillings, and those I can't just let you have."

Brenner understood Knoll excellently now because he was speaking loudly and clearly—and had suddenly switched to, let's say, a more informal mode of address.

"Either you sign now or you find yourself another chump who'll buy this barracks off you for five times its value. Do you think I came all this way with a notary so that I could haggle over eighty-three cents?"

"What's 'five times the value' supposed to mean?" the Schrebergartener protested. "Supply and demand!"

Shameless people always believe that all people are as dumb as they themselves are shameless. And maybe the shamelessness of the hard-of-hearing house-seller infected Brenner a little, too, because by now he'd ventured far enough out to the tiny staircase that he could see the three heads below through the brittle railing above. Interesting, though. Knoll: bald. The notary: thinning mousy hair. And the pensioner, of all people: full head of white hair. And the notary was even fairly young. But mouse hair already! And the skin on Knoll's crown was peeling a little. Brenner thought to himself, *amazing that he doesn't take better care of himself in the sun*, and he thought about maybe bringing it up with him if a good opportunity arose.

The white-haired pensioner was finally signing now. Because it might have become clear to him that he shouldn't wear out his patience with Knoll and the notary, and so before the buyer could change his mind, he'd put his three X's down on the contract and left with the envelope of money.

It must have been an interesting sight that morning for the nosy neighbor of Knoll's new premises. Forty-nine hours after the disappearance of Helena Kressdorf. First the pensioner limps out the door with a thick envelope and doesn't even close the garden gate behind him. And shortly thereafter a taxi pulls up—because the outermost row of the Schrebergarten lets directly out onto the access road—and the notary with the briefcase climbs into the taxi, and right after the notary, Knoll comes out and gets in his Volvo, and half a minute later Brenner leaves the house. Caravan: understatement.

And if the neighbor had looked very closely, she might have even noticed that Brenner was following Knoll in his purple Mondeo—car chase, if you will. But she couldn't possibly have guessed everything that Brenner had yet to face that day. Even with the most ironclad resolve, Brenner himself couldn't have guessed. And to be perfectly honest: if he had guessed, he wouldn't have driven one centimeter after Knoll. Because Brenner would have preferred to stay in the Schrebergarten cottage, prayed a few Our Fathers, and searched for a rope to hang himself with in peace.

CHAPTER 12

Mankind could not have invented anything better than driving a car. Especially when you have someone you can follow. Because then it's not so boring. The constant looking in the rearview mirror just made Brenner realize how often he would check to see if Helena was okay when he was driving, if she needed something, if she was sleeping, if she was smiling, if she was sitting comfortably, if she wanted a sip of something, if her teddy bear had fallen over, if she'd care to discuss something, or if she'd like to have her peace and quiet.

And every time now, no Helena in the rearview mirror. It pained Brenner so much that he even let out a cry. Because that's one of the many advantages of a car. You can listen to music in private, you can enjoy nature without exertion, and when in despair, you can let out a cry.

For the sake of the car chase, of course, it was good that Brenner's rearview glancing should plummet so dismally into emptiness. Because, he was all the more sensitive to what he saw behind that emptiness. Never before had a detective tailed a suspect as attentively as Brenner did Knoll—from the rearview mirror. Because he always left enough distance, and where Helena's face would've been in the rearview mirror, Knoll's black Volvo was gliding along in the back window, but very tiny. The best music Brenner had heard in years was on the radio, the sun was laughing, traffic was rolling smoothly along, and it annoyed him at first when the programming got interrupted. But then, of course, believe it or not, the dead-serious news announcer reported that the case of Helena Kressdorf's kidnapping had taken a dramatic turn due to a bloody incident with the ransom handover.

And you see, that's the downside of driving. Because you think you're the only one experiencing something, you think the world stands still while you're in motion. But in reality, you're the one sitting with one foot on the gas pedal and the other on the clutch until the radio tells you that the outside world just turned in a bloody direction.

So what happened while Brenner and Knoll were rolling merrily down the autobahn like two innocent children on the Lilliput train pretending to be cops and robbers?

Listen carefully. You need to take note of the following: the difficult thing about a kidnapping is always the ransom handover. If that weren't true, everybody would be kidnapping everybody else. It would be paradise on earth! Imagine, no one would have to work anymore; instead everyone would make a living purely by kidnapping. You wouldn't have to do anything to the kidnapped victim—treat them well even, better meals than at home, warm room, color TV, everything, and as soon as I have ten million in my account, he's free to go home. It wouldn't have to be a major drama. On the contrary, maybe he'd even go home with some spiritual gains.

Unfortunately, the handover, though. That's where things went awry. The worm is simply always inside somewhere.

And so there you have it. Train, highway overpass, remote-controlled things, and, and, and. Always the unlikely endings, alas, where the kidnapper hunts a police squad through the city for days, from phone booth to phone booth, from message to message, pointless merry-go-round. That never pays off! I say, when you're the kidnapper, and you steal time from the police for days, then you can't be surprised. Because that young cop's got a girlfriend, he'd also like to go home and watch TV, another one's got a second job as a security guard, he loses the extra pay, or the single mother has to skip out on her appointment with the child psychiatrist all because of your ransom money handover. Naturally these public servants are going to become aggressive.

Prime example, the husband of the nanny who Brenner always dropped Helena off with and picked her up from. He came up with the idea of making his wife's nursery school the ideal place for the handover. Because the middle of a group of children, of course, not so easy for a sharpshooter. Flip-side of the coin: he's all the more nervous. And you see, that was the moment when Brenner lost radio reception. You should know, they were just racing past Salzburg, i.e., the German border—you barely notice it these days. So they're already over the border, more or less, and in the middle of the report about the kidnapping, the signal switches over to Bavaria 3. While Brenner's frantically dialing around on an unfamiliar radio, he loses Knoll from the rearview mirror.

To this day I'd be interested to know whether he lost Knoll merely because of that—because Knoll heard the report, too, and slowed down to search for better reception.

Now for some brief, general considerations until they

get the station back. The proof that you actually have the kidnapped victim is child's play today compared to how it used to be, i.e., forensic evidence. It used to be that a finger would have to get hacked off, an ear, a toe, it was a dreadful burden for victim and perpetrator alike, because you don't just go cutting off someone's finger no matter how desperately you need the money. And today a hair suffices, a fingernail, and it makes it that much easier for all involved.

Easier and more difficult! Because nothing in the world's got only advantages! And the great weakness of forensic evidence is the sidecar driver. Because DNA's a real man-about-town. And one thing you can't forget. A finger, an ear, that's a one-of-a-kind matter. But a few hairs you can easily pluck off a piece of clothing or a comb, even if you don't have the kidnapped child at all. Especially if you're the husband of the nanny. And when on the same day that his unemployment benefits got cut, he read in the paper that the kidnappers hadn't made contact, he simply plucked a hair off the sweater Helena had forgotten there.

Brenner was just hearing all of this now that he was finally able to tune the station back in. He nearly bit the steering wheel when he learned that Helena still hadn't been found fifty-two hours after her disappearance, but that the nanny's affable husband was dead on account of a nervous sharpshooter. Imagine, just a few days earlier Brenner had stood out in front of the building with him while he had a cigarette—because in the apartment, of course, strictly no smoking, don't even ask.

But I have to say, for a lowly sidecar driver it wasn't the stupidest idea. Listen up: the children his wife looked after were supposed to take a field trip on International Savings Day, and the money was to be placed in one of their little backpacks, i.e., swap-on-the-way, tiny backpack full of cash for Helena. That was his objective, ostensibly, when in reality he'd quietly taken the money out of the backpack for himself back at home before the group embarked. They caught him in spite of this, of course, and no way would he have been able to run because, old saying: *well intentioned is the opposite of well kidnapped*.

Or better put, of well blackmailed, because he didn't kidnap anyone. But I say they didn't have to go and shoot him, although I can understand that the police were nervous with so many children playing. That many children would make anyone nervous—even without a kidnapping. Brenner felt somewhat complicit because he was the one who'd forgotten the sweater at the nanny's a few weeks ago. Well, not really forgotten, more like intentionally left behind, because he'd never liked the sweater. But maybe he was just using his guilt to whitewash his despair over the fact that Helena was still missing.

The announcer reported further information and an interview with the head of the police operation, and Brenner got incredibly annoyed when just ten kilometers past Walserberg, he lost the Austrian station for good. Suddenly, Knoll passed him out of nowhere, and the Mondeo nearly started bucking on the autobahn just to catch up even halfway to the black Volvo. He wondered whether Knoll had heard the radio broadcast, too, and he wondered where Knoll was headed, why he was driving in the direction of Innsbruck, and he hoped that any additional radio reports would come on only after they were out of the German triangle again, and he prayed he wouldn't lose the Volvo.

Knoll exited the autobahn at Wörgel, and you could learn a lot about the human brain if you were to analyze Brenner's breakdown here. I think he just didn't want it to be true that Knoll was headed to where he was headed. But his behavior was becoming rather textbook now, and textbook: always a bad sign. He said to himself, *Bundesstrasse, better if I stay behind him because it's better not to follow from ahead in the mountains*. He thought about these kinds of things, you see. Then he dialed around the radio again to see if there was another announcement somewhere. He had to have said to himself, *I'm not interested anymore, it was just a sidecar driver, it does zero for Helena, I'm casting it aside*. But that's how people are. Always backward. Then he thought of her forgotten green sweater again with the green duck embroidered on it—terrible! And it seemed to him that Helena hadn't liked the duck, either. All of this, just so that he wouldn't have to face facts.

When Knoll turned off just five kilometers before Kitzbühel, things got stressful for Brenner. And I don't mean the stress of being stuck behind a truck at a red light while the Volvo pulls ahead. I don't mean the life-endangering stress of overtaking the truck and racing ahead, either. Because he had the Volvo right back in his sights. But then Knoll turned again. Brenner didn't like that at all. When Knoll drove up the private street that Brenner knew so well.

There was just one more thing for Brenner, of course. He had to take the cutoff through the woods. He'd taken it once before in Kressdorf's jeep when the access road had been closed due to a mudslide, because two weeks of constant rain set off a mudslide that even made it onto TV, and the eternal optimists, immediately hopeful: *finally the lord god had a revelation and was cleaning up Kitzbühel.* The road through the woods hadn't been a problem for the jeep back then, but it bordered on miraculous that the Mondeo was able to withstand the trip without breaking its axles. And Brenner even imagined Helena's guardian angel watching over the Mondeo's axles, because otherwise, inexplicable. You should know, Brenner drove like the devil. And when he finally came out up at the Hegl Mountain Inn, he could still see where just a hundred meters below, Knoll was parking in front of Kressdorf's house.

And believe it or not, Knoll knocked on the door. And the man who came out and warmly greeted him, fifty-four hours after the girl's disappearance, was Kressdorf.

CHAPTER 13

In hindsight it came to this: why didn't Brenner? Because it's always simple in hindsight. I like how the clever people went and criticized him of all people, though, when the whole thing never would have gotten off the ground without him.

And besides, what was he supposed to do? Call the police so that he could get arrested again? Or pound on the door with his own fist and say, "The game's up"? Or climb onto the roof and storm down the chimney like some kind of Santa Claus in order to free Helena?

Those people, really, I could just partially—. And from his parking spot at the Hegl Mountain Inn, he had box seats. The Kressdorf cabin gleamed in the sun—no match for van Gogh—except his view of the two cars was cut off by the cabin. The most brilliant sun wouldn't have done him any good. But nothing was stirring around the cabin anyway. Nobody came and nobody went. It's no wonder then, that as the time wore on, Brenner became more aware of the impressions streaming in at him from his immediate surroundings. Namely, the magnificent aroma coming from the restaurant at the Inn. Nobody thinks of that, either, that Brenner hadn't eaten anything all day. As a detective you're supposed to resist everything, and in hindsight that means: Why didn't he? What was he supposed to do?

He quickly got himself something to eat from the Inn, and before anybody gets excited: in those five minutes absolutely nothing happened. And while he was eating his bacon rolls in the Mondeo, nothing happened, either. And then nothing happened for another hour. And then another hour and nothing happened. The Inn closed and the waiter drove off. The sun slowly made its way down toward the mountain peaks, the cabin cast an increasingly ominous shadow, and Brenner began to grow nervous that he'd have to spend the night there.

It's interesting, though, what looking off into the distance can do to you. It simply affects the thought process. A monk or a hermit can spend years doing something like this, and you can only imagine how much they must experience if a few hours is enough for Brenner's question to be suddenly freed of snow in his mind, like after a long hard thought-winter: *why did the Frau Doctor have Congressman Stachl's cell phone number?* And so you see once again how unjust the unconscious can be. Because the mistrust that had sunk its teeth into Brenner ever since he saw how friendly Kressdorf had been in greeting Knoll was now spreading to his wife, and what was she doing with Congressman Stachl's cell phone number at all?

You're going to say, *my god, business crony, guest at the house, so the woman has his cell phone number, or maybe her husband gave her the number for emergencies, maybe in her panic she'd called the congressman's office and gotten the number.* You see, you're exactly like Brenner! He was telling himself that, too, now to put his mind at ease, *my god, business crony*, and so on. But when a question like that washes to the shore of your consciousness, you don't get rid of it that quickly. You look away briefly, and then look back again and—it's a little strange that she sent the congressman a text message. And so you toss the question aside again, but when it comes back yet again, you know you need a better answer.

As Brenner was looking down at the cabin below, where it was still completely quiet, he thought about whether he should call and ask Natalie. Or even Peinhaupt, because he'd mentioned during the interrogation that the poor mother hadn't been able to reach her husband at first, and even then it was via the congressman. Brenner didn't think anything of it yesterday, because when you're wading deep in feelings of guilt, you don't ask a question that concerns the child's mother, of all people. And even now he shoved the question aside, but then—*I could ask Harry*. You should know, Harry was Congressman Stachl's chauffeur, terribly fat, for years he was the driver of the mayor of Vienna, but when there wasn't room in the car for two anymore, he got decommissioned to the slim congressman. Brenner had talked to Harry two or three times at the MegaLand construction site, a pleasant enough person, but he didn't end up calling him now after all. Namely, because he didn't have Harry's cell phone number, and you see, there was that question again: *why then would the Frau Doctor have the congressman's cell phone number when I don't even have Harry's?*

I don't know where you stand on things like telepathy. Personally, I'm totally against it, pure nonsense if you ask me. Is it supposed to get transmitted over the airwaves or something? How do people imagine this working? But if I ever let myself get talked into believing in it for at least one second, then case in point—Brenner's looking down at the cabin, has no idea what Knoll's talking to Kressdorf about, and voila, this question occurs to him. A person gets to thinking.

In hindsight, of course, it gave Brenner something to think about, too. But he couldn't have known at the time that the two of them were inside the cabin just then, discussing the very question that was going through his head, too. And he didn't have any more time to preoccupy himself with the question, either. Because fifty-seven hours after Helena's disappearance, the black Volvo suddenly rolled back out onto the street and drove down into the valley. Brenner expected the jeep to soon follow, but nothing doing, the jeep didn't stir from its place.

Then the worst thing that can happen to a detective happened to Brenner. Fifty-seven hours after the girl's disappearance, he became innocent. Which is awfully dangerous in a situation like this. And when you, the detective, begin to sense that you're innocent, then it's only right that you rehash ten times whether you'd convinced yourself of things just so you could justify taking action. And one thing you can't forget: due to the personal shock, due to the pangs of guilt, even Brenner was in danger of making a move too soon. He convinced himself that he'd seen Kressdorf sitting in Knoll's Volvo earlier. Then he pulled himself back together, because how's the naked eye going to recognize who's sitting in a car from this distance?

After half an hour he couldn't stand it anymore and

drove down. He hid the Mondeo in the wooded bend before Kressdorf's driveway, then crept around the cabin three times. Heart pounding, don't ask, because it had been a while since he'd done something like this—and no more guns since the pills because the lawmakers had said, *it's wiser if you give us back your gun license.*

Just to be on the safe side, he knocked, because he'd have to come up with something if Kressdorf opened the door. But nobody opened it, nothing moved at all. The jeep was still parked in front of the house, but Kressdorf wasn't there anymore.

Fifty-seven and a half hours after his little ward disappeared from his car, dissolved into nothingness, dematerialized in her car seat, got swallowed by the Zone of Transparency—Brenner only needed half a minute to climb up over the wooden balcony and into the cabin. And while he searched the lavishly appointed cabin for Helena, while he searched the living room, searched the rabbit pen, searched the upstairs bedrooms, searched the closets, searched the bathroom, with every centimeter that he searched, he became more depressed. Interesting, though, how often depression will send you searching for false assignments of guilt! At this point Brenner wasn't connecting his depression with his fear of finding Helena dead, because he didn't dare think that far ahead yet; instead it was the cabin that was to blame. Brenner escalated to full-blown cabin rage now. Everywhere you go, these cabins, Schrebergarten cottages, mountain houses—why can't rich people just live in normal palaces? There was once a revolutionary who said, *War on the Palaces, Peace to the Cottages*, his slogan, as it were.

He'd like the look of things today. Because these days, when rich people are caught up in such a house-frenzy, where the largest businesses snap up the ski and beach and mountain houses, he'd have to say: *War on the houses!* And everyone who inhabits a farmhouse or a mountain house or any kind of house—but the only calluses on their hands from playing golf—take up your torches!

Brenner stormed out into the fresh air with rage in his belly. But there was no relief outside either. And certainly no reason to take a deep breath. The insects descended on him, reminding him of his conversation with Knoll about the gnats. They let loose on him like he was crossing the most poisonous river, say, the Jordan. Especially back behind the moldering shed it was completely black with gnats, maybe because of the rotting wood that Kressdorf had deliberately left there, because he said, *it has a certain flair, the original*, and *don't just renovate everything to death*. But Brenner couldn't see much of the ornamental decay because there was nothing but gnats and more gnats. And the longer he searched, the more flies that joined the gnats. More and more flies and more and more hornets and more and more gnats. He imagined this being the right track now—where there were more and more flies and gnats, then his friends, the flies and gnats, would lead him to Helena.

But behind the shed door that hung on rotting hinges, no Helena, beneath the shed's outer steps, no Helena, in the firewood bin, no Helena. He turned every woodpile over, all but reaching into the molehills. He slowly began to realize that the insects were leading him in circles. Here and there he'd make a point of walking away from the gnats and flies and searching off on his own. Even though he knew for a fact that he had to be inside the swarm for the gnats to lead him, not out on the flowering meadow.

But easier said than done of course, when your greatest fear is that in searching you might find something. He stepped off course again now, away from the foul recesses where the squadrons of insects wanted to lure him, out to the yarrow, out to the chrysanthemums, out to the spignel. To the burnet, to the white clover, to the lady's mantle. Out to the devil's claw. He was so exhausted by his fear about Helena at this point that he lay in the grass and thought about how easily he used to deal with the basic questions surrounding death. How he used to have a good handle on the hereafter when he was a young man.

There are many schools of thought on this, and I tend to say you shouldn't spend too much time thinking about it because it won't get you anywhere. Brenner was different. Early on he'd staunchly believed that the most beautiful women would want to know whether you were one man for one brief life, or whether they could count on you in the afterlife, too. And so he developed a staggering sense for which answer would make the best impression in any given situation. For a time Asian beliefs were in demand, and reincarnation all the rage, then back to everything being contained somehow within nature as a whole, then you'd be well served by the shamans again. There were also those who needed a challenge, though, so Brenner said, *alas, there's nothing on the other side*, because with them it got you farther than if you guaranteed them a heaven.

And believe it or not, just a few weeks earlier, he'd tried

that route with Natalie. But alas, just the painful realization that the old recipes weren't working so well anymore. He thought he could provoke her with a few quotes from Knoll's brochure, i.e., when does life begin? He spited himself nicely with that one, though, and he came to understand right away that Natalie stood head and shoulders above him. She had considered the problem in such a balanced way and had such an understanding of the opposition that it was almost too much for Brenner. *It's difficult, of course*, the psychologist said, *to determine the exact day when you can safely say, up until this point, it can still be removed because it's not a person yet*—well, soul and all still negligible—*and from that point on, it can't very well be removed anymore, because it's already too much of a person and even a hint of a soul.*

The insects tried every means of shaking him awake and forcing him to get up. They stung him and tormented him, but he wasn't quite ready yet, he wanted to escape a little further into this nice memory. Of this good conversation and how he'd answered Natalie that it's difficult everywhere in life to draw such exact lines. For example, in criminal cases there's always this type of development, too, at first it's harmless really and not an actual crime yet, you think about it only theoretically, who you'd have to kidnap if you were to do it—a party game, as it were. And then you contemplate how the ransom handover would have to be arranged, still not a crime yet. And then maybe you do a little prep work, buy a good roll of tape at the hardware store—still not a crime yet—and finally, tidy up the basement. That, too, still isn't a crime yet.

But then there is the one step where you can't go back

anymore, where you can't dismiss the reality anymore, where you've got the child irrevocably in your stomach or the kidnapped victim irrevocably in your basement.

The insects made Brenner understand that he couldn't go back anymore either now. He'd come along like a man sentenced to death. Nothing else could help him now. He's already here, he's got to finish it, too. And so the searching takes on its own dynamic entirely, and even if you hope you don't find anything, you keep searching. He was escorted by the gnats, which he didn't really notice anymore. Just like you stop noticing your bodyguard over time—he's just there, and he simply must have been there when Helena was kidnapped—so, too, the insects buzzed around him now and directed him along the west side of the cabin toward the driveway. The wood still retained the warmth of the sun and smelled terrifically good, the old wood that the cabin was built from, the wooden beams, the wooden shingles, the planks of the balcony, the railing on the stairs, the window frames, and the firewood, but the bleached wood lining the driveway smelled best, i.e., the age-old boards that covered the cesspit.

When Brenner removed the first board, of course, it didn't smell so good anymore, because a cesspit like this greets you with the stench of many generations. And with the stench came swarms of gnats, climbing out from the slats between the boards, you can't even imagine, as though the collective dead or unborn humanity were lurking there beneath the rotting boards for Brenner.

You're going to say, *why would the gnats take Brenner under their wings, what's their motive?* Because for the average gnat, a human murder isn't the least bit interesting, and even if you believe all that—before life, gnat, after life, gnat—then it bears saying all the more, as far as of one of these eternal gnats is concerned, a human murder's the least interesting thing that there is.

Look, my take on it—think what you want! All I know is that as Brenner searched the cesspit for the corpse by the light of the evening sun, he was surrounded by an almost supernaturally glowing aura of insects—half beekeeper-at-sunset, half Jimi-Hendrix-in-a-spotlight. And who knows, maybe Jimi Hendrix was only lit up so ethereally in those colorful hippie photos because the spotlight was fractured into millions of invisible festival insects that were already luring Jimi, at the age of twenty-seven, toward the exit, without anyone in the audience noticing.

From Brenner's point of view, of course, nothing was illuminated at all, just black clouds rising from the cesspit, because that's how it is in the physical world, solid matter, liquid matter, gaseous matter. And maybe from a distance it looked nicely lit and sparkling in the last rays of sun, but to Brenner it looked as if the brown sauce in the cesspit was transforming from liquid matter to flying matter. The swarms of gnats rose out of the cesspit but didn't fly any farther. Instead, there just seemed to be more and more of them the longer he stared into the pit and hoped that it wouldn't turn out badly for him.

He took a pitchfork down from the shed and poked around in the brown soup with the handle, not with the tines. Let's be honest, though, if someone was down there, it really wouldn't matter, handle or tines, but somehow it goes against something, purely some inner code, to jab a person with a pitchfork. At any rate, Brenner had the pitchfork flipped over and was poking with the handle. He noticed right away, though, that the pitchfork was too short and couldn't reach the bottom, but just as he was about to give up and look for something longer, he hit something that felt suspicious, a strange resistance, half hard, half soft.

You can picture it for yourself now, and I'll leave out the grisly details. I'll just say that without the pills he would have lost his mind by now, at the very least. Although the corpse was still completely covered with, with, with . . . He couldn't get a good grip on it, instead, picture it like this: someone with a pitchfork struggling against a sludge-covered underwater monstrosity. And at that moment, when Brenner realized that it wasn't going to work any other way, when he flipped the pitchfork over and began jabbing at the corpse with the iron tines, and when, with his left foot at the very edge of the pit, the shit started seeping into his shoes, he heard a voice.

The voice of Jimi Hendrix. Brenner took his cell phone out of his pocket, and believe it or not, "Unknown Caller."

"Brenner?"

That he even answered the phone, of course, can only be explained by the fact that in an extreme situation like this, man brings everything to bear on himself—epicenter of the world, as it were. And it wouldn't have surprised him if, on the other end of the line, the good lord himself had laughed into the phone while observing Brenner through a telescope from his hiding place.

"South Tyrolean shpeaking," a woman's voice said into the telephone.

It took at least three seconds for Brenner to switch gears. Probably because he was struggling so hard to keep the slippery corpse from slipping right away from him. With his left hand now he simply reached into the putrid sauce while holding the cell phone in his right, but still his wires were crossed. Even though the voice said, "South Tyrolean shpeaking," and not "It's Monika," because then it would have been excusable for him not to recognize it, or even more than excusable, it would have been understandable, because he had no idea that the South Tyrolean's name was Monika. But even so, when she said, "South Tyrolean shpeaking," it took him half an eternity.

At that moment Brenner was overwhelmed by the greatest feeling of happiness of his entire life. But not because of the South Tyrolean. Because at that moment he realized that it wasn't a child's body. You should know, fifty-eight hours after Helena's disappearance, Knoll's face came bobbing out of the mud.

"From the gas shtation," the South Tyrolean said, trying to jog his memory.

He looked at Knoll desperately, as if maybe he could explain to Brenner how the South Tyrolean got his number.

"Or do you go shouting your telephone number out after every woman you meet?"

But it was all he could do to keep Knoll and his cell phone both from sliding into the cesspit, and you can't be angry at him for not having a good line at the ready. He really couldn't believe what an uncanny memory she had for numbers.

"What's wrong with you?" the South Tyrolean asked.

"Why, what would be wrong?"

"You sound like you jusht saw the devil."

"Why would the devil show his face to me?"

"Maybe this isn't a good time? You're gashping like you're—"

"Why wouldn't I be gasping?"

Then Brenner puked into the cesspit, but don't go thinking that he at least hung up the phone first. No, the South Tyrolean was allowed to hear everything beautifully, and she asked him, "Did you jusht throw up?"

"Why would I throw up?" Brenner asked.

"There's shomething important I need to tell you."

Brenner would have preferred to tell her to keep it to herself, that important something. Because he'd never liked it when a woman started off with, *there's something important I need to tell you*. It's always, every single time, something unwelcome! And you always have to act interested because otherwise it instantly means: *or are you just not interested?*

"Or are you jusht not intereshted?" the South Tyrolean asked.

"Tell me."

"I hope your phone hashn't been tapped."

Brenner began to tremble, out of fright that Knoll was dead and out of relief that it wasn't Helena, so much so that he wasn't really listening to the South Tyrolean anymore.

"Because I did in fact see shomeone that day."

"This just occurred to you?"

Now she was the one who didn't answer.

"What did he look like, then?"

"I'm not talking about a he. It was a she."

It seemed to Brenner like Knoll's face was grinning snidely at him. But that wasn't the reason why he dropped him back into the cesspit. Because let's be honest: what else was he supposed to do with him?

CHAPTER 14

Sixty-three hours after Helena's disappearance and just before midnight, Brenner stood in the South Tyrolean's doorway, and immediately, she rolled her eyes. And believe it or not, Brenner rolled his eyes, too. Let's be honest, great love stories don't usually begin this way, but the eye rolling was warranted, and in fact, both sides were fully entitled.

Brenner rolled his eyes because he could barely make it through the door on account of all the plants—"gardening" doesn't come close. And she rolled her eyes because Brenner still gave off a residual whiff of cesspit, even though he'd showered for fifteen minutes in the cabin's swank bathroom and then put on a fresh set of clothes from his duffel bag. And before you ask what he did with his dirty clothes—he threw them into the Kitzbühel Ache River. But the stink must have settled somewhere deep in his pores, or else the South Tyrolean simply had an acute sense of smell. Her description of the woman at the gas station was the opposite of acute—exactly as vague as his whiff of cesspit. Approximately all the women in the world were brought under suspicion. No height, no hair color, no nothing. And as for the child, she wasn't even a hundred percent certain whether there'd been one.

"But she wasn't a man—that you're sure of," Brenner grumbled. Because he was starting to get the suspicion that she had lured him over under false pretenses, just because she was getting bored without a newspaper.

"You think I don't have eyes in my head?"

Brenner didn't say anything to that, because first of all, he was far too tired to argue, and second, the South Tyrolean had cooked him such good midnight spaghetti that he nearly fell blissfully asleep at the table. Because South Tyrolean women: always good cooks. And when, after three plates of pasta, Brenner felt more pregnant than any patient who'd ever shown up at the abortion clinic, the cook even offered that he could spend the night. Not what you think, though! Because the South Tyrolean made it abundantly clear to him that he shouldn't misunderstand her.

"*Woascheh,*" the South Tyrolean said to Brenner, but it was in South Tyrolean and really only meant, "You know, eh?"

Brenner understood it, no problem, because a classmate of his at the police academy was from Sterzing. Ladinig was his name, always won all the executive ski championships, and an avid mountain climber in the summer, driving home every weekend and mountain climbing. Interesting though, it wasn't in South Tyrol where he crashed, but on the Matterhorn. Two weeks after their graduation from the police academy. Ladinig had always used the catch-all "*Woascheh,*" too, and so Brenner was able to understand the South Tyrolean now without any trouble.

And interesting: after just that one word he knew truly everything, and she wouldn't have to explain in any detail why the topic of sex had long been, and would always be, off-limits for her. She wouldn't have to open up to Brenner about how, during her early active years in South Tyrol, she'd already completed a comprehensive study of this science. Brenner would've understood, too, if she didn't want to list off every fire department, every music festival, every small town disco, every teacher, every priest, every church choir director, before coming to the conclusion that "Tyrolean men are such emotional halfwits, you can't even imagine."

That surprised Brenner, because Ladinig had been one of his nicest classmates, beloved by women and everyone else. Personally, I can't fathom how the Tyroleans could be such losers and brutes, but that's exactly how Monika saw them. I think if she'd happened to grow up somewhere else, maybe she would've blamed it on that region, but she never came down off it, the Tyroleans in general and the South Tyroleans specifically—coldhearted Pinocchios.

Brenner didn't even attempt to turn her argument around on her, along the lines of, *I'm a graduate of Puntigam's Elite Sex University, where the Kama Sutra comes from*. And here you can see how exhausted he must have been to leave something like that out. Although, to be frank, since the pills, he hadn't been all that interested anymore, and strictly speaking, he wouldn't have needed Knoll's death as an excuse for why he preferred to sleep alone.

The apartment was half the size of South Tyrol, on the ground level of an old building across from the gas station, cheap and dank and loud and all, but enormous. In spite of this, he wasn't allowed to choose which room he got to sleep in, because she told him he should just take the first one if he was so afraid of plants.

"And besides, this way you won't be far from the bathtub. Did you shwim in sewage?"

Brenner declined the warm milk with honey that she wanted to prepare for him—world-renowned South Tyrolean sleeping pill—because, on principle, no milk. And I have to say, the South Tyrolean was even looking at him a little amorously because it was a commonality that seemed terribly meaningful to her. With a certain pride that women often resort to when they can tack a minor health deficiency or nutrition problem onto their breasts, she explained to Brenner that she didn't even have the enzyme necessary to digest milk. She couldn't impress Brenner any more tonight, though, because he was already so tired that the word "enzyme" sounded like something inflammatory creeping into his ears.

He only sat there as long as he did because the few steps to the bedroom seemed insurmountable to him. And one thing you can't forget—the plants kept growing all the while. What he really would've liked was to ask the South Tyrolean for a machete. Somehow the room came to him, though, and really he would've liked to just let himself fall into bed. Her comment about the smell had already grabbed hold of his pride, though, and so, with his remaining strength, he overcame the philodendrons and fought his way into the bathroom.

He slept so deeply that the next morning he didn't know where he was. For a moment he thought he might have drowned in the cesspit like Knoll, slipped in while he'd been on the phone, fell on his head and straight up to heaven. You should know, it had been years since he'd felt refreshed upon waking up. He lay there so delicately covered, bundled, and swaddled, all in clean white, where a man might get to thinking, *you see, you could live like this if you bought into marriage*. And it wasn't just the bedding he was covered with that was white but also the bed frame that cradled him on all sides like he was a newborn. Or let's put it this way: Brenner was just now realizing that he'd fallen asleep in the bathtub last night, and slept so soundly that there had been nothing else for the South Tyrolean to do but cover him up right there in the tub.

A human soul has never traveled quite so fast from heaven to hell, though. Because Brenner was also just realizing why he'd woken up. The cell phone in his heap of clothes was ringing, and he would have given anything in the world for it to be "Unknown Caller." But it was no unknown caller. Believe it or not, seventy-one hours after the disappearance of her daughter, the Frau Doctor was calling him.

Twenty minutes later her BMW was pulling into the gas station. Because that's where Brenner had told her to go—not very sensitive I have to say, but in his grogginess he couldn't come up with anything better than the gas station across the street.

Brenner stood there dumbfounded a moment before opening the passenger-side door, because the idea of the Frau Doctor sitting at the steering wheel and he getting into the passenger seat seemed very strange to him all of a sudden.

"The car's the only place right now where I don't have the feeling that I'm being listened in on," she said in greeting.

"By the police or by the kidnappers?"

Brenner had never seen a person change so much in

three days. Except for someone getting an arm or a leg shot off, that's always a sudden change, or slipping under a bus, both legs gone, something like that's a sudden change, too, of course, but right after that would come Frau Doctor Kressdorf's change. Because she must not have eaten a bite since the day her child disappeared, and even that doesn't explain it, either, because—completely different type of person. If there is such a thing! It even looked to Brenner like her hair and eyes were a different color, but not what you're thinking: dyed. No, like they'd really changed.

Character-wise, absolutely unchanged. And that was a huge relief to Brenner right now. No hysterical outbursts, no embittered remarks, not even a sigh or an accusatory look. Brenner was profoundly impressed by her self-control. She was utterly calm as she drove downtown, no aggressive accelerating, no abrupt brake slamming, no accusatory gear shifting, no demonstrative temperature adjusting, no frantic windshield wiping, no nervous window opening, no sacrificial-lamb turn signaling, no lane changing where it wouldn't have been advisable to do so, and where the sensitive passenger and child-loser might've detected a sighing rebuke.

Brenner thought to himself, *other families who've been affected by kidnappings should really look to her as a model.* Not always making things more complicated, because when you've been affected by a kidnapping, you see it as your great hour having arrived. *Finally, the big chance and now it's my turn for once, now people will indulge all of my whims, and now everything around me will have to pay until it doesn't know which way's up anymore.* Brenner had experienced this more often than not in his days on the force. Because the motto of families affected by kidnappings: *the police will pay for everything that's ever been done to me in life.* And families affected by kidnappings wield power, you wouldn't believe it, they drive doctors, psychologists, and social workers to suicide—ergo, all new victims of kidnappings.

"I have to tell you something," Frau Doctor Kressdorf began abruptly after driving for a full minute in silence. But then she fell silent again, and it was only as she was turning onto the Ringstrasse that she found her words. "There's something I can't tell the police. If you can't, or won't, keep it to yourself, please tell me right now."

"No problem. No one will hear anything from me."

He would've liked to have said that with a little more conviction, but personally I think a dry promise isn't the worst, because how do you prove to someone that you won't tell someone else? It basically only applies to your best friend anyway, who'll probably tell his wife the very same evening, who'll solemnly swear not to tell anybody else, and her best friend will have to swear the same thing half an hour later. The more adamantly a person vows to keep a lid on it, the more certain you can be that, come tomorrow, the entire world will know. And you see, Brenner said it just that dryly, and he's probably the first person in the world who's never actually spoken a dying word of it to anybody. These are the things I like about Brenner. But since it's just us, I'll make an exception and tell you what the doctor said.

"I've done something that I could go to prison for."

"You?"

Pay attention: if one of the advantages of driving is the freedom to shout openly, it only applies, of course, to when you're driving alone. So why is Brenner shouting so loudly now when he's sitting right next to the Frau Doctor:

"You?"

And what kind of a shout was that? A shout of surprise? A shout of rage? A shout of pain? I'm tempted to say, all of them together. Surprise, because naturally he expected her secret to involve her husband, the Construction Lion, who'd lured Knoll out to his house in the mountains. And rage, because he sensed that she'd already decided, before she even began her story, to withhold half of it. And pain, I don't even need to explain to you, when you're speaking for the first time with the mother—who looks like she's aged thirty years in seventy-two hours—of the child you lost.

"Yes, me," the doctor answered softly, and got honked at from behind for the crime of not stealing into the intersection while the light was still red.

Her confession of guilt made Brenner feel completely hopeless. Because one thing you can't forget: nothing derails a manhunt more effectively than a self-afflicted guilty search party that constantly holds up the investigation with its self-blame.

Brenner would've preferred for her to tell him something about her husband. But the Frau Doctor didn't have much of a clue about his construction business. That's often how it is, that you don't know exactly what kind of business your spouse actually does, main thing, the money's there, main thing, the villa's there, main thing, the park's there, main thing, the yacht's there, main thing, the staff's there, main thing, the art's there, main thing, the charity thing's there, main thing, the therapist's there, in other words, the most important things have got to be there, it's got nothing to do with your own standards, my god, you could live a much more modest life by yourself, you could get by with a smaller villa, with a smaller park full of smaller trees, too, with a smaller yacht, with smaller paintings—and if you must, even with smaller charity things—but for the child it would be a pity indeed to grow up in cramped conditions, and that's why it's important for the family estate to be established a far cry from the poverty line. But now I'm talking as fanatically as Knoll, this kind of thinking's contagious. You've got to be careful not to go sympathizing with Knoll all of a sudden just because he landed in the cesspit of a Construction Lion.

For a second there Brenner thought, *the Frau Doctor knows what happened to Knoll, and she wants to tell me.* He asked her very cautiously whether she believed there was a connection between her law violation and the kidnapping, and the Frau Doctor, completely calm and matter-of-fact, said, "I don't know. In my situation, you believe everything could be connected with it."

"We've all broken the law at some point," Brenner said, purely out of discomfort.

But he was already thinking that she probably wasn't talking about driving too fast, parking illegally, listening to loud music after midnight, vacuuming on a Sunday, or walking off with a pretty sweater from a boutique back when she was a med student.

"Terminating the pregnancy of a twelve-year-old girl."

"Is that illegal?" Brenner asked, in an effort to cover up his relief that she wasn't mixed up in Knoll's murder.

"It depends."

"You probably did it for the child."

Already you can see how Brenner's bad conscience had put him more on the side of the doctor than on the side of the law. Or not just a bad conscience, but sheer masculine sympathy for the doctor, too. And from a professional standpoint, it's always better with confessions to give the confessor a good feeling. "Confession comes from comprehension"—they hammered that one right into him at the police academy, i.e., interrogation rule number one, if force doesn't do anything.

The doctor gave him a look that made it clear she would refuse any and all excuses. Some people are so incredibly stubborn, they want the kind of guilt that they can hang on to and never let go.

"I meant to say, you must have done it for the twelve-year-old girl," Brenner explained. Because suddenly it occurred to him that his remark—that she'd done it for the child—might have come out wrong, that maybe the Frau Doctor had thought he meant that she'd done it for the aborted child; that possibly, purely out of self-flagellation, she'd thought Brenner had referred to the aborted gnat as a "child."

"The girl was poor," the Frau Doctor said. "At first she didn't tell anyone she was pregnant, and then it was too late. But I wasn't supposed to do it. Not anymore by that point. And not before, either. Not without reporting it."

They were coming back around now to where they'd first turned onto the Ring. And on this second lap around, the whole thing seemed like a hand over situation to Brenner, where the kidnapper demands, *drive around the Ring until you receive the next instruction*, i.e., a tactic to wear you down. And maybe that's why you see so many cars here, day and night, driving in circles, because everybody's waiting for their kidnapper's next instruction.

"I don't want to justify it to myself, either, that there are countries where it's legal." The doctor's voice snapped him out of his thoughts.

"On the other hand," Brenner said, because the Frau Doctor looked so crestfallen that all he wanted to do now was console her.

"On what other hand?"

"On the other hand"—it's always bad to begin a sentence with "on the other hand" when you don't know what you want to say after that—"it wouldn't have done anybody any good if the abortion had waited any longer," Brenner stammered. "How many months along was she when she came to you?"

"We calculate in weeks, not months."

That was her entire answer.

"Got it. There used to be a saying: ten months but no cash on delivery."

Brenner thought he could lighten up the mood a little, but the doctor hardened at his remark, and it wouldn't have surprised him if she'd driven straight to the Hotel Imperial.

"I just meant," Brenner said, "if they were that poor. Twelve years old and life already screwed up. You've got to help. You can't just force morality about becoming a mother on a child like that. Women used to die because of illegal abortions!"

"I didn't come to you for consolation," she interrupted

him. "My problem is that I can't tell the police. I was even prepared to. But my husband's convinced that this is exactly what Knoll set out to accomplish."

"Knoll knew about it?"

Brenner was starting to feel like he was riding a merry-go-round as the palaces along the Ringstrasse went past him again, the Opera, the Hofburg Palace, the Parliament, the Burgtheater, and down to the Mint again, to the Ring Tower, around and around in circles. Or a few laps around the Lilliput Rail, but for some reason, instead of trees they passed buildings, and for some reason instead of Helena, it was her mother who sat beside him, and for some reason instead of being happy he was—how shall I put it—devastated would be an exaggeration; more like numb.

"My husband turned to Reinhard, and Reinhard advised Knoll not to use his evidence. Or else he'd call his loan due. We'd looked it up in the Land Registry—which bank Knoll was keeping the money in that he'd bought up the other units in the building with."

Defense Ministry, Museum of Applied Arts, City Park, Schwarzenberg Square, Opera.

"I've wished ever since that he wouldn't have let himself get cowed by Reinhard. Then that maniac wouldn't have taken my child away from me."

Brenner shot her a look like she was only telling him half the truth. But he couldn't very well call her on it. He wasn't telling her everything, either; quite the contrary, he even asked her now whether she'd heard anything from Knoll in the meantime, i.e. intentional misrepresentation.

"You know what I think?" she said, while they were stopped at a red light at the Schottentor for the fourth time.

"Knoll is calmly waiting for me to go to the police myself with this story about having illegally terminated the pregnancy. Then I'll be ruined professionally, and he'll send Helena back to me." Her voice faltered for a moment, but she kept impressive self-control—not even half a tear. "And he's accomplished everything without making himself known. He'll be rid of me without ever making contact with me."

"It really wouldn't have been badly orchestrated," Brenner had to admit. "But most of the time criminals aren't thinking about it from so many angles." He couldn't exactly tell her that Knoll was dead. Drowned in the cesspit behind her own house.

Instead he just pulled out the photo that Knoll had given him. "Was this your underage patient?"

The Frau Doctor looked at Brenner as if he were Knoll himself.

"Do you know where she lives?" Brenner asked smoothly.

"Where did you get that photo?"

Brenner shook his head. "Surely you have her address somewhere."

"You really don't get it! I don't want you to find this girl. This isn't about her."

"So where does she live?"

Approximately one centimeter before a jingling streetcar crossed the tracks, the doctor yanked on the steering wheel and came to a stop at an empty taxi stand in the adjacent lane. She gave Brenner a look as if to say, the entire conversation had just been sadistic foreplay leading up to this second when she was going to eat him alive, the man who'd managed to misplace her child.

"I get it, you don't want to put your patient in a difficult position. That it's purely about Knoll for you. But the direct route doesn't always get you anywhere," Brenner explained to her, and shocked himself by how consistent this was with the truth according to Knoll. "Often it's only through the detours. Our professions aren't so different on this score. Doctors ask, too, whether you have cold toes at night when you go to them because of a headache. And those are opposite ends of the body."

"Which you don't know everything about."

"That the head's on the opposite end of the body than the toes, even non-doctors know that."

But the next moment nearly saw Brenner and the Frau Doctor become Vienna's latest criminal case. Because a furious taxi driver pounded on the windshield, and if Brenner hadn't immediately locked the doors from the passenger seat, everything would have been over, guaranteed. He suddenly had an inkling of what Knoll's last seconds must have been like, because unfortunately the passenger-side window was open a crack, and the atmosphere inside the car changed because of the killer cabbie, as if the entire car were sinking into a cesspit.

Interesting, though: the attack was good for the conversation, because as they drove off in a hurry, their conversation popped back into gear.

"I don't know the girl's address. I don't keep any records of my crimes."

"And she doesn't have a name, either?"

"I only really know her first name. And even that she told me in an immigrant's Viennese. How the kids talk who are born here but speak another language at home."

"Oida! Oida! Oida! Oida! Go shit I say!" Brenner thought he could impress the Frau Doctor with how well he could imitate this throat malady. Maybe elicit a small smile in the midst of a desperate situation.

"You do that very well," she said, but not with a smile; no, so coolly that despite the 77-degree weather, the windshield-washing fluid would've frozen, guaranteed, had he not just refilled the antifreeze a few days ago. Under better circumstances an even wittier reply would have come to him. But stricken as he was, he only heard hurtfulness in her remark. He only detected from it that she counted him among *them*, her staff; that he was the sort who, right from the outset, never had a chance in his life with someone like the Frau Doctor, because of education, because of age, because of manners, because of language, because of money, because of everything.

"And her first name was probably fake, too," she continued. One thing you can't forget: for her, the remark had been no big deal. She really did have other concerns. "Maybe it was just a nickname: Sunny."

"Probably short for Susanna," Brenner said, because he couldn't help but think of the Susanna who'd once won the grand prize at the Linzer police department's Christmas raffle, believe it or not, a ski weekend in Hintersoder for two, and no one was allowed to call her Susi—only Sunny.

"Short for Susanna," the doctor replied, "I don't think so. Susanna isn't a particularly common name among immigrant girls. I think it's more likely English."

And Brenner, with particularly good pronunciation, "The sunny side of the street." Not sung, of course, just spoken.

"Sunny side," the doctor repeated pensively, as though she had to think about what it could possibly mean.

"I once paid for a young woman's abortion, too," Brenner began, hoping that with this story he'd get somewhere with the Frau Doctor yet. "In my police academy days. Her name was Hansi, short for Johanna."

"Aha."

"It was still illegal at the time, so she drove all the way to Amsterdam. I paid for all of it. Train, hotel, abortion."

"And you went with her?"

"No, I didn't have enough money. Two train tickets, then staying overnight, plus meals on top of that. But in hindsight I have to say, it would've been cheaper if I had gone. Because she changed her mind in Amsterdam."

"She discovered herself with drugs instead."

"Not drugs, exactly—hashish. And after a fun week she returned without the abortion."

"So you're a father?"

"Was."

The doctor looked at him with utter sympathy, and Brenner saw the old Frau Doctor in her again, the one who was always personable and friendly.

"Two years she let me pay alimony, but then the finance director in Graz married her. She was the type that men chased after. Although to be honest, I have to say, I only liked her from the side. But the finance director took her nonetheless."

"Maybe he liked her from the front, too."

"No, I meant he married her in spite of the kid. And after the wedding she admitted that the child hadn't been mine at all, but another classmate's from the police academy. He probably paid for the abortion, too. But the alimony, only me, because my classmate died on the Matterhorn before the child was born."

Seventy-four hours after her daughter's disappearance, the Frau Doctor began to cry because of this story. Brenner apologized for mentioning his classmate's death. But she said it was okay, her nerves were just fried, and really she should be the one to apologize for burdening him with her story. And you see, that's another similarity between the medical profession and the detective profession. Because just like patients will often change their minds in the waiting room, *my tooth doesn't hurt after all*, so too did Helena's mother lose her courage, and instead of wanting any more help from Brenner, she just wanted to be rid of him as soon as possible.

Brenner felt so sorry for her that up until the moment when he got out of the car, he'd been considering whether to betray every shred of common detective sense and tell her that Knoll was dead. And you see, that was exactly the wrong question. Because really he should have been asking himself why her voice changed so suddenly, why she revoked her trust in him when he told her the story about the police academy. If he'd just tugged on these flimsy strings, the entire solution probably would have presented itself, and five people wouldn't have had to die.

But maybe the time simply wasn't ripe yet, seventy-four hours after the disappearance. Because one thing you can't forget: the Zone of Transparency doesn't tear open until the fifth day, i.e., one hundred hours, at the very earliest.

CHAPTER 15

Between the seventy-fourth and the eighty-eighth hours, Brenner did some first-rate investigative work that was never fully appreciated afterward. It all got overshadowed by the next day's madness. Obviously, with a development like this, the detail work gets lost. The carpenter can't bid personal farewell to every wood shaving with a thank-you speech for the top-notch collaboration, and once a crime really gets escalating, when a murder is paid a visit by its little children, the subsequent murders, then a detective can't be praised for everything that he did right.

But because everyone glossed right over it, I'd like to at least touch on it briefly. I have to say, it was brilliant how Brenner spearheaded the search for the Yugo-girl. For Sunny. He achieved peak detective form there, and there's only one thing to be said: hats off.

I don't get it either. It's a sign of our times that nobody properly appreciates these things anymore. The clean detective work, the police procedural, the craftsman's skill, none of it has any worth today. Even Brenner himself didn't think anything of it, or didn't look back proudly on it later. Because it is what it is, and what it is is his job. And I can understand it somehow, too, how he didn't pat himself on the back; how, even though he was exhausted from his encounter with the Frau Doctor, he still managed to drum up the only people who could get him in the door of the Yugo-scene. And how he tracked down Milan, freshly fired from the gas station, home in front of the TV, and sent him through the Yugo-disco circuit with Sunny's photo. Milan was thrilled about his new assignment. The only touchy subject was when Brenner asked whether he could maybe get hold of a gun. Brenner hadn't meant any offense, along the lines of, anyone who sells beer out the backdoor can get hold of a gun, too. He just didn't feel completely at ease anymore since he'd discovered Knoll. But that was also the only mistake he made that day, everything else first-rate.

For Brenner, things were going exactly like they would for everyone else afterward, which is a way of saying, what happened to him would radiate out to everyone else that night. But we haven't gotten nearly that far yet. Because seventy-seven hours after Helena's disappearance he hired Milan, and seventy-eight hours after Helena's disappearance he already had two liters of weak Schrebergarten coffee in his stomach, half a kilo of powdered sugar in his blood, and twenty Schrebergarten scandals in his thick skull. Among them, though, was the explanation for why Knoll had bought the cottage. Believe it or not, his attorney had filed a neighbor's injunction against the MegaLand project—in other words, immediate halt to the construction.

Eighty hours after Helena's disappearance, Brenner picked up pills for his headache at the drugstore, and as soon as they started working a little, not quite eighty-one hours after Helena's disappearance, he called Kressdorf and disguised his voice, posing as a journalist who was hoping to find something out about MegaLand's halted construction. Interesting, though: Kressdorf wasn't impressed one bit and was even quite confident that the injunction wouldn't hold for long.

He didn't get anything more out of Kressdorf, and I have to say, it's for the best. Because otherwise maybe Brenner wouldn't have wrung from his frustration the courage to call Natalie, too. And he really did learn something from Natalie. Or better put, from the truth written in flames. But for now, pay attention.

Eighty-three hours after Helena's disappearance, Brenner persuaded Natalie to meet him. At first she was rather rigid and resolute in her claim that she couldn't explain why the Frau Doctor would have Congressman Stachl's telephone number, either. Of course, there was no reason why she should be able to explain it, that's true enough. But why would Natalie get so red in the face while saying so, like a shy girl who was telling a lie for the first time in her life?

"The Frau Doctor came to me today," Brenner said, "even though she shouldn't have, if it's a police matter."

As he spoke, her rosiness faded again but only from her face. Because the red spots on her neck darkened all the more. It looked to Brenner as if the truth which hadn't escaped Natalie's lips was searching her neck for an emergency exit.

"She talked to me for hours"—he wasn't cutting Natalie any slack—"but I sensed that, at the last second, she didn't trust me with the secret she'd actually come to me with."

The red flames spread from her collarbone to her jaw

now, as if the intrepidly silent Natalie were hastening her body to write the truth in flames on her neck so that she wouldn't be forced to say it aloud. But I always say, a truth written in flames is written in haste. But you've got to be able to read it right. And just between us, Brenner had no grand gift for language. You could write something out for him in flames, and he wouldn't understand it. He just stared at it long enough until Natalie took it upon herself to spell it out for him. Because, "written in flames," what's that mean? Written in blood, you'd have to say. After all, it was the blood that pushed itself to the surface of her neck, and blood was exactly what this story was about, when she finally came out with it. But pay attention now, because this gets interesting.

Natalie told him that Kressdorf's and his daughter's blood types don't match. My dear swan, the heat was even rising to Brenner's head now. Adrenaline surge: understatement.

"I don't understand why she hasn't told the police," Natalie erupted. "If it were a matter of my daughter's life and death, I'd tell them everything! They tried artificial insemination for years because Kressdorf's sperm quality wasn't good. We learned about it at the clinic. And then all of a sudden she was pregnant!"

"Right around the time Congressman Stachl started showing up around the clinic?"

"Why are you asking me, if you already know?"

"And Kressdorf? Does he know?"

Natalie shook her head. "The Frau Doctor would often cry on my shoulder back then because she was so done in by the hormone treatments. She had eight failed attempts altogether. Do you know what that means for a woman? And then suddenly she was pregnant."

"And you suspected the truth from the start."

"No, mostly it just surprised me. I didn't suspect anything at all. I was honestly happy for her. And the thought never even would've occurred to me, if our receptionist wasn't always coming up with a new diet every few months."

"The blood-type diet."

You're surprised that Brenner knew about this fad. Simple explanation: the receptionist had tried to convert him to the blood-type diet his very first week on the job. He didn't tell Natalie this now, though, because he didn't want to interrupt her explanation.

"Our receptionist asked each of us what blood type we were. For a few weeks there, until she came up with the next diet, everyone knew each other's blood types. The Frau Doctor was A, and her husband A, too. But, no one asked which blood type Helena was. I'd noticed back when she was born, though, that she was the same as me. But a child can't be type B if both parents are A."

"I don't know offhand which blood type I am," Brenner said, and maybe you can tell from his pointless comment that the story was starting to get on his nerves.

And maybe, too, he wanted to spare Natalie from having to say, "I can never forgive myself for letting it slip to the receptionist. I impressed upon her that she could not, under any circumstances, tell anyone else, but you know how that is. I have no idea how many people know about it now."

"Knoll, anyway."

Interesting, though: Natalie turned an entirely different

shade of red now than before. And that's why I say the red spots on her neck were really meant as a message from Natalie's unconscious. What else are you supposed to do when you're the unconscious? You can't talk out loud, as Natalie now did when she asked Brenner, "Do you think it has something to do with the kidnapping?"

"No clue."

And I've got to say, Brenner had seldom been so right. Within just a few hours he would become all too conscious of just what little clue he truly had at that moment.

But for now, pay attention.

CHAPTER 16

These days, everybody knows the standard links between sex life and human life, where it's typically thought that the one arises from having done the other—causal relationship, as it were. Not just causal, but a temporal relationship, too, because the one's always nine months before the other, or maybe even eight or seven months. A pro-lifer would even say, a single day after the former and you've already got the latter. But nobody would dispute that, strictly speaking, the one's always got to come before the other. No one would claim that a special exception can be made and it can happen the other way around—credit at the sperm bank, as it were—and you've had your kid two, three years already before you find a five-minute window in your planner to quickly do the sex part for your progeny who's already making prettier drawings than the other children in kindergarten.

You see, they haven't invented that yet. It's been going on for long enough without any personal contact—i.e., porno mag and a reagent cup—that they have it well in hand these days, but even that doesn't work the other way around, where you've already been on vacation with the kid twice when one day the collection letter comes that you're finally supposed to sire the child. No, everything's got to wait its turn: first beget, then have.

Just so you understand why Brenner was so shaken up when suddenly it did get reversed. Because what he was about to experience on this night, no man before him had ever lived to tell; on that I'll stick my hand in the fire.

Watch closely: around one in the morning, after the South Tyrolean had placed another plate of the world's best midnight spaghetti on the table, and after Brenner had fallen deeply and soundly asleep on a full belly and within five seconds was dreaming about some police academy nonsense, the South Tyrolean hopped into bed with him.

I don't know, there are often different rituals with women—one says this, another says that—and the South Tyrolean belonged strictly to the group that says: *with me, not a chance, bed, sex, case closed, and especially not with you.* And when, as a man, you completely understand that, when you're tired yourself and happy to be crawling into a freshly made bed, when you're already falling asleep, when you've possibly already been the best wife to yourself, when you're blissfully dozing off—that's the moment she crawls into bed with you, and the rules don't apply anymore because she's changed her mind.

And quite energetically in fact, the South Tyrolean. I've honestly got to say, she awoke a young Brenner within the old Brenner. But maybe the sudden change of heart wasn't the South Tyrolean's doing alone. I could thoroughly imagine it being his fault. Because one thing you can't forget: since finding his way back onto the detective track again, Brenner was exuding a completely different magnetism.

You're going to say, by now Brenner's already put the longest day of his life behind him—he'd looked the Frau Doctor in the eye, he'd called her husband, he'd read off of Natalie's neck that Stachl was the father of Kressdorf's kid, he'd ventured into the Schrebergartener's lair, he'd found Milan and hired him to find Sunny, he'd done more police work in one day than some of his colleagues had in their entire civil service careers—and so he's allowed to say *let me sleep* without his honor as a man being at stake. And even if you've slept in a guest bed ten times, you're allowed to turn down even the best hostess, midnight spaghetti or no midnight spaghetti. But no chance of that, because the secret behind her surge of energy and his newly raging detective hormones weren't having it. Believe it or not, when the South Tyrolean came to him, he didn't even cry for help; on the contrary, he said to himself, *why not, we're not getting any younger*.

Now surely you still recall the trend that was once popular among tennis players where they'd let out a powerful groan with every stroke. At the time, my dear swan, people said, the way tennis players exult over every ball could put thoughts into even the most respectable person's head. But here we go again with the before and after. Because these things can flip themselves around like desperation on a surveillance video, and all of a sudden now—as the South Tyrolean grew more and more animated—Brenner thought of televised coverage of women's tennis. And while the South Tyrolean took ever greater delight in her guest, every possible name of tennis players he'd seen on TV ran through his head, the Czechs were good for a while, the one was lesbian, and the other was even named Hantuchova, now he was just thinking about her, about Hantuchova—when all of a sudden the door opened, and eighty-eight hours after her disappearance, Helena stood in the doorway crying.

"Aw, you're awake, *Schatzele*!" the South Tyrolean said tenderly and pushed her long red hair back from her face.

Brenner would always remember the faint electric zap as one of her strands of hair left his sweaty neck. Otherwise, complete mental standstill for Brenner. In a situation like this, of course, when you're lying in bed and had been asleep before, you can easily escape into the hope that you're dreaming. But for how long? Two, three seconds? After that, Brenner played for time a few seconds more by contemplating whether it wasn't just alcohol that was forbidden while on the pills but sexuality, too—ergo, side effects, e.g., hallucinations—and he was just imagining that little Helena was standing in the doorway crying, imagining that there were rivulets of tears running down her upset face, as the South Tyrolean said, "Aw, come here, *Schatzele*. Did you have a bad dream?"

And you see, that's what I wanted to say. Before they were even halfway done with the sex part, Brenner and the South Tyrolean were already lying in bed like the happiest married couple with their child. And believe it or not, Helena fell asleep on the spot, because there between the South Tyrolean and Herr Simon was as good as anywhere. The bit of sleeping pill that the South Tyrolean had put in her milk before putting her to bed was having a slight effect still. And because I'm talking about milk: I don't know whether this stood out to you, but it was definitely taunting Brenner now that he'd overlooked it. The South Tyrolean had explicitly told him that she didn't drink milk, she couldn't digest it, she didn't have the enzyme, and what did she buy the first time he met her at the gas station? A liter of milk! He'd wondered about the newspaper that she bought but didn't read. But the milk he'd let slip right past. And so you see how often we very nearly miss things in life, because you go looking to the newspaper when the interesting news is right there in the milk.

"Well, now you know that I took her," she said quietly. "But only because you left her sitting there in the car for hours on end. In the heat! If you'd done that to a dog, there'd be a national uprising and a warrant out for your arresht."

Brenner's heart was beating with such relief that he didn't hear what the South Tyrolean was saying at all. He was just amazed that Helena could even sleep when just a few centimeters away, his heart was beating like a baby dinosaur that was about to hatch out of his chest and greet the world. But the beating was so loud and so rhythmic that no such musical dinosaur could exist, Brenner thought. It sounded like it had swallowed Jimi Hendrix's drummer, Mitch Mitchell, and he was playing "Foxy Lady" in honor of the red-haired woman in bed.

You know what's interesting, though? When Brenner really did lose his mind out of fear eleven hours later, he didn't fully realize it. But, for now, he lay there with a clear mind, watching Helena sleep and thinking to himself, *so this is what it's like when you lose your mind.*

The pills probably helped save him from the brink. Because eighty-eight hours after Helena's disappearance and a few minutes after her reappearance, the pills in him said:

these things just happen in life. And as you've already noticed, the pills reassured him, *the South Tyrolean is a little strange. My god, she took the child. Better than if someone else had taken her. She just borrowed Helena for a few days. "Borrowed" or "born," they sound so similar that it can't be that bad. You hear time and time again*—the pills floated before his eyes—*about women who don't have children sneaking into maternity wards and snatching newborns. And anything that happens over and over isn't not a little normal,* the pills in Brenner argued. But the dinosaur in his chest said, *Here I come!* But the pills said, *that can't be a dinosaur, because—too musical, it must be Mitch Mitchell, who, out of thanks that you dedicated the PIN to him, is playing "Foxy Lady" for the South Tyrolean.*

You should know, it was the pills that were holding Brenner's mind together. And he didn't actually lose his mind. He listened to his heart's drummer drumming his heartbeat the whole night through and thought about what he should do now. And about why Knoll had landed in the cesspit if he had nothing to do with the kidnapping. *How is it all connected*, he asked himself, while Mitch Mitchell wouldn't, wouldn't quit hammering his foot into Brenner's chest. He simply didn't, didn't get tired, and Brenner couldn't, couldn't stop thinking.

What had Knoll wanted from Kressdorf? Was he just another sidecar driver like the nanny's husband? What had Kressdorf wanted from Knoll? Do Reinhard and Congressman Stachl know that Knoll is dead? Does Kressdorf know that Helena isn't his? Brenner was riddled with so many questions but never, never the answers.

My god, "Foxy Lady"'s three and a half minutes should be

long over by now, he groaned. But Mitch Mitchell played on till morning. He simply wanted to prevent Brenner—after Jimi Hendrix and after Noel Redding and after himself, too—from cashing in his chips before his time. The downside to such a vigorous heart massage, of course, is that there can be no talk of sleep. Helena was sleeping, the South Tyrolean was sleeping, Brenner couldn't sleep. Couldn't, couldn't. But you'd think an answer to his questions would've occurred to him at least, like Helena's accidental kidnapping and Knoll's death being connected. But it didn't, didn't. And didn't, didn't. And didn't, didn't.

CHAPTER 17

It was shortly after four when Brenner finally stopped thinking. But don't you go thinking he fell asleep or died. No, instead of "Foxy Lady," Mitch Mitchell switched to "Castles Made of Sand" all of a sudden—in other words, Milan was calling Brenner's cell phone. You've got to picture this: it's after midnight, you're lying in bed with a South Tyrolean, and before you can really get going, the kid shows up, and a few hours after that, Milan's calling you, too—straight from a Yugo-disco. Because he'd found Sunny.

"If you ask me, she'll be back there in no time," Milan explained to Brenner.

But he didn't understand. Acoustically, sure, understood, cell-phone-wise a first-rate connection—unheard of—but strictly brain-wise, it didn't fully compute. You can't forget, half an hour earlier the South Tyrolean had forced another glass of warm milk with honey on him because the sound of his grinding teeth kept waking her up. *Warm milk with honey is the besht sleeping pill in the world*, she'd proclaimed yet again. But as for the actual sleeping pill that she'd put in his milk, she didn't say a word. And right about now when it's starting to take effect, here's Milan on the phone.

After everything that had happened, it seemed to Brenner like the call luring him out to the Yugo-disco at four in the morning was stretching him to about eight feet. And Brenner had never been the tallest, so you couldn't say, *eight feet doesn't mean a whole lot because your average medieval rack in the rec room could manage that.* The phone call was pulling his head in the Yugo-disco's direction, but sleep was pulling his feet in the opposite direction.

And so you see how a person's mind can get a little dull when it's stretched too far, because—with the South Tyrolean in his right arm and the cell phone in his left hand and the child's snoring in his right ear and weariness in his bones and medicated sleep in his veins—Brenner couldn't understand what Milan could possibly mean.

"What does that mean, 'she'll be back there in no time?'" he murmured into his sweaty pillow.

And Milan said, "If she keeps on like this, she'll be pregnant again in no time."

"Aha," Brenner said, excitement tugging on his hair and the sleeping pill tugging on his leaden toes.

"But nothing to worry about," Milan said.

"Nothing for you to worry about, or nothing for her to worry about?" Brenner asked.

"Nothing to worry about. Because in three months she'll be fourteen," Milan said. "Then an abortion won't be a problem anymore."

"Right," said Brenner.

"Or at least it won't be a problem for her boyfriends."

Okay, that last bit wasn't on the phone anymore. The excitement had yanked him so hard and the sleeping pill, thank god, had surrendered—otherwise Brenner would've been torn down the middle, like that fabled child whose two mothers pulled for so long that the child broke in half, and ever since there's been man and woman—in other words, the eternal struggle over surrender. Brenner didn't break in half, though. Instead, he sprang out of bed at four thirty in the morning and sped over to the Yugo-disco so he could talk with the girl.

He didn't have to speed at all, though, because Sunny was still dancing like a wind-up toy when he got there. There was nothing left for Brenner to do now except for what men do best at a disco, i.e., drink beer and gawk.

"So what's her real name? Where did you find her?" Brenner asked.

When someone asks two questions at once, there's always a third in the throat. Because you have to wonder, *what's behind it, why did he ask two questions at the same time?* Well, I'll tell you two things. First, Brenner was far too tired to go breaking his head over old police academy wisdom. And second, it was about to get much worse, because Milan answered with yet another question now.

"Do you like lasagna?"

"Lasagna? Do they have that here?"

"No, that's her name. If you drop the 'la.'"

"Sagna? Why can't you just say it normally? Simple: 'Her name is Sanja,'" Brenner suggested.

"If I say Sanja in this noise, you'll hear Tanja," Milan yelled in his ear. "But if I say lasagna without the 'la,' then right away you understand Sanja."

Milan looked stern yet sly, like one of those natural healers who condemns you to death for coffee or alcohol or enjoying life.

"Not bad," Brenner answered. "So where did you find her?"

"Here," Milan said.

"Where?"

"There!" Milan yelled and pointed with his index finger to somewhere vaguely in front of his feet. It was so loud now and the music was so good that even Brenner's foot began to tap a little.

"There?" Brenner yelled back. "Like 'over there' without the 'over'?"

You see, just before complete catastrophe, right before the world ends, there's often a moment when human beings are in the mood for one more joke. But, okay, Brenner couldn't have known, per se, about catastrophe and the world ending. And Brenner wasn't thinking about what came after yet, but about what came before, i.e., whether it had been a terrible mistake to leave Helena in the South Tyrolean's care till morning. Should he have brought her to the police immediately? Should he have notified the Frau Doctor right away? Could it possibly be a horribly bad sign that not even ninety-two hours had passed and the Zone of Transparency was already starting to rupture even though the fifth day had not yet begun? He thought about this while he watched Sanja dancing and Milan talking, because he could only hear Milan when he shouted directly into his ear.

Sanja danced with a stamina like she wasn't interested in anything else in the world, and Brenner began to wonder whether she would ever stop.

"What did you mean by that?" he yelled into Milan's ear.

"What?"

"What did you mean by what you said earlier?"

"Yeah, I'm not deaf! But what did I mean by what?"

"Her boyfriends who it won't be a problem for. What did you mean by that?" Brenner yelled a little softer.

Milan pulled one of those free daily newspapers out of his bag, and the newspaper reminded Brenner of the South Tyrolean the first time he saw her, when he'd only paid attention to the newspaper and not to the milk. He was almost certain, too, that the South Tyrolean wouldn't pull any nonsense. Almost. Almost completely certain. The South Tyrolean's intentions weren't bad. He was almost certain. He'd promised her that after all this was over, he'd help her out in court. So that she'd walk away from it with probation. And she wasn't completely crazy, not technically. Instead, more of a mixture of opportunity offender and—. Almost certain.

Brenner tried to calm himself down by thinking the same thoughts over and over, just like Sanja made the same moves on the dance floor over and over. He needed to justify over and over to himself, it was pure impulse, as if things would only go well for so long, as long as he could convince himself that enlisting the kidnapper as a babysitter for a few hours would be an acceptable solution in an emergency—community service instead of prison, as it were. And what else was he supposed to do? Because as soon as you get a kidnapped child back, the biggest question right off the bat: *where am I going to get a babysitter now?*

"The guy who got her pregnant," Milan said.

"What about the guy?"

"For a detective, you're awfully slow." Milan casually pointed to the newspaper page he'd opened up in front of him.

It was an article about MegaLand that Sanja's aunt had given Milan. You should know, Sanja's aunt was Zivka, who was from the Lovreć area, and Milan's sister's husband, Dusan, was from Katuni. And Dusan's cousin Cvetanka was from Kresovo. And Cvetanka went to a trade school in Lovreć with Zivka's little brother—well, not with Radan but with Todor. And that's how Milan found out that the girl in the picture is Darko's cousin. And from Darko he learned that his mother, i.e., Zivka, had just showed him a photo in yesterday's free sheet, where her niece—so, his cousin Sanja—had squarely and firmly claimed that the man in the photo was her rich friend.

Brenner gathered from the article that the construction of MegaLand was nothing but advantageous for all involved. Because the jobs, the tax revenue, the infrastructure—all for the general public. Quite remarkably, the Lilliput Rail extension, which was slated to run around the MegaLand Discovery World and down to the Greenland Schrebergarten, had been canceled. And Schrebergarten residents would each get a free parking place in the underground garage as a gift.

Brenner started sweating a little when he read that. Believe it or not, of the four people in the photo, he knew three: Kressdorf he recognized right away of course, Congressman Stachl and Reinhard right away, too, because it hadn't been that long since he'd seen them in Klosterneuburg. And the fourth was a high-ranking Vienna politician, who I have an agreement with not to identify him by name. You'll have to take my word on it because—sources.

Milan casually gestured at the photo with his chin and said, "Him there."

"Which one?"

"The one on the end."

"Left end or right end?"

"Edge of the page," Milan said and checked how his sunglasses were sitting on his head, he wore them like a headband, don't ask me why.

"That sick bastard!"

Milan didn't react to Brenner's outrage, and in fact, he looked so coolly at the dance floor that it was as if he hadn't heard him cry out at all. And Brenner was probably the only one anyway who was surprised by his outburst, because as I've said, since the pills—often spontaneous emotions. They simply came out of him like hiccups or opinions do for other people.

And maybe it was only to calm Brenner down just then that Milan said, "I got hold of a gun for you."

He said it as casually as if he were telling Brenner about the gas station's latest offer of a free cookie.

"That fast?"

"Yeah, but not a real one," Milan said.

"What's 'not real' mean?"

"A toy gun that looks one-hundred-percent real. Better than nothing," Milan said.

"That's worse than nothing!" Brenner felt his anger rising all over again.

But he pulled himself right back together, because Sanja was finally making her way over to them. She ordered a Diet Coke, and she was sweating so much that Brenner almost told her not to drink her Coke too fast or else the ice cubes in it wouldn't cool her down. You can't forget, Sanja reminded Brenner a great deal of Greenspan, Renate, who'd sat next to him in school for six months because they'd put him next to a girl as punishment. Of course, Diet Coke wasn't around yet back then, just regular Coke, or rum and Coke, but otherwise, Sanja: pure Renate. Everything, the hair, the nose that would've been the envy of every Indian chief, and then those eyes. I'll just say this much—Renate's last name was actually not Greenspan but Haller. Greenspan was a nickname, cf. eyes.

He'd only really gotten as far as he did in high school because of Renate, even though his grandfather would have held a place open for him at the mechanics' school, and to this day Brenner was still sorry that he hadn't become a mechanic. But Renate was such a good student that his note taking alone improved, and then on to the next grade at school, and then the police academy instead of mechanics' school, just how life plays out.

Milan was telling Sanja some story about Brenner needing the address of where to get an abortion for an underage girl. She in turn gave Brenner a look that was just like the look Renate always used to give him, but he wasn't sure whether Sanja was spurning him because he was a man who had gotten a young girl pregnant or because he was a loser who didn't know where to get an address for a thing like that. Because despite her youth, Sanja's pretty Renate-eyes revealed a certain worldliness, and Brenner could read in those eyes that she'd never be so stupid as to let herself get taken advantage of by a loser.

Milan must have noticed, too, that Sanja wasn't exactly laying a good groundwork for conversation with Brenner, because he explained to her now that Herr Brenner was the grandfather of the pregnant girl. Milan meant well, but Brenner was a little insulted because he thought "father" would have sufficed, "grandfather" was an exaggeration. But "a little insulted" was only his initial reaction. Because within seconds the insult had worked itself into the wildest frenzy. Grandfather! There went another one of those emotional hiccups that he'd sometimes felt since the pills and that wouldn't stop now. In order to distract himself, Brenner ordered another beer, but when he pointed at his beer, he saw that the bartender hadn't given him a nonalcoholic beer before, even though he'd asked an extra two times whether they had nonalcoholic beer. And he felt so angry at the bartender that he would have liked to smash the bottle right over his head.

And you see, that was the itinerant rage. It's a survival reaction—just like the body falls over when too little blood goes to the head, anger travels when you're about to burst. It's purely for release, you have to picture it like an athlete who always rotates which muscle group he's working out. And once it hits a certain magnitude, peak rage needs to be constantly rotated, just like overworked muscles, so that the person carrying the rage doesn't explode—in other words, the rage has to get rolling. The rage strolls from one circumstance to another, from one person to another, from the man in the newspaper to the man behind the bar, from the bartender to Renate, from Renate to Diet Coke, from Diet Coke to the music, from the music to Milan's sunglasses, to anything that you see or hear or smell—a rage that rotates is a rage you won't choke to death on.

And believe it or not, the alcohol and the pills and the despair and the exhaustion and the memory of Knoll in the cesspit and of Kressdorf opening the door to Knoll and offering him a friendly hand, and above all of Reinhard—his magnanimous thousand-euro benefactor, who spends his nights in his domicile and his days in his refuge and who can currently be identified in the photo in the newspaper—filled Brenner with such rage that he didn't know any other recourse. And for the first time since he'd fought with Renate over some stupid little thing, Brenner went out onto the dance floor, just so he wouldn't have to look at haughty Sanja with her Renate-face any longer.

Brenner was a terrific dancer, the likes of which you've never seen—everything that has ever moved to music between New York and the Yugo-disco is just a limp-chested chicken dance by comparison, because Brenner was an elemental force. But the Yugo-kids didn't understand and started leaving the dance floor one after another—in protest, if you will.

And when he returned to the table, Milan and Sanja were gone. He didn't find them outside, either, and not at the entrance, not by the coat check, not at the bar, not in the bathroom. Sanja had disappeared. And when Brenner's itinerant rage took square aim at himself now—you can't even imagine. At first at himself, but then at Milan. When he nearly bumped into him. Right next to the men's bathroom, by the delivery entrance. Now, even though it was only just getting light outside, Milan had his sunglasses right on his nose. But Brenner could tell from a single glance that he was dead.

CHAPTER 18

It had to come to this, though. When you've got Knoll murdered in the cesspit, then it's safe to assume that somewhere, his murderer is running around. And you can't expect him not to care, when day and night you're thinking about why Knoll landed in that cesspit. Well, just thinking about it's okay. But asking around, poking around, rummaging around Schrebergartens, newspaper photos, Yugo-discos! That kind of thing makes even the most well-tempered murderer nervous.

And when the murder victim is lying in your former boss's cesspit, and when, shortly before his murder, he brought about a halt in construction to your boss's biggest development project, and when, before his murder, he was still the main suspect in the kidnapping of your boss's child, and when, on top of that, you saw your boss personally greet the murder victim in front of his house—then you can't be surprised. So, of course, a few minutes after finding Milan, Brenner was lying in the trunk of a car, tied up as tightly as for a seafarer's burial, and being transported to god knows where.

Interesting, though: even if you can't see anything at all, you try to orient yourself somehow anyway. *Where are they taking me?* As far as your senses go, you haven't got a chance in a trunk, of course. In a situation like this, when you can't see anything, and you can't hear anything either, except for traffic noise, you have no choice but to venture a good guess. You've got to gather your wits about you with a vengeance and bravely settle for a hunch—straight out of your head and into the blindness. And only afterward can you say—from how well you intuited the jolting, the turning, the braking and accelerating, the uphill and downhill—okay, hunch, right or wrong.

Sir had taught them that many years ago, their only instructor at the police academy to always wear a suit, and for that they nicknamed him Sir. They'd laughed at Sir back then, because that was a time when people were saying, *just the facts, we're not interested in anything else*. And I'm apt to say, as long as the facts work, I'm fully in favor. But, in the dark, of course. In the trunk. With your eyes blindfolded. Blind like an embryo. Brenner was experiencing firsthand now how, in such godless darkness, you can't look to the facts too much, and you can't endlessly analyze the vibrations, either, because—it's hopeless. Sir had been completely right about this: you must first start with the guess, the hunch, the maybe, the probably, the possibly. And Brenner's the prime example of this right now. *They wouldn't take me to Kitzbühel* was his first thought in the trunk. That was actually more of a fear than a guess, but pay attention to what I'm about to tell you: a fear is also a guess.

So just when his fear had ventured this guess, it also seemed like the vibrations from the braking and accelerating and turning were confirming his suspicion. Or at least not disproving it! And don't forget how well he knew the route. *That could be the traffic light just before the on-ramp to the autobahn*, he guessed, *it's always so ill-timed that if you want to make the second light up ahead, you need a rocket launcher. And that could be the off-ramp now*, he guessed, when he got slammed against the side of the trunk so roughly that the centrifugal force nearly broke his neck. He hadn't guessed anything else yet, of course. Namely, how much he'd be wishing in just a few hours that the centrifugal force really had twisted his neck. But no such luck, neck-wise Brenner took after his sturdy grandfather, in other words, his neck held out easily.

Then the car straightened out so fast and clean and suddenly, it was like Brenner was a suitcase in a spaceship being hurtled into the next galaxy. You also have to be careful with blind guesses, though. Under no circumstances may you succumb to the intoxication of a blind guess and adopt an anything-goes stance—from a spaceship to I don't know what. Instead, always stick with the most probable variant, and you see, here the facts come back into play. Because *if they've thrown me into a trunk, then I can't suddenly be lying in a spaceship now. Much more likely: autobahn.*

They were on the autobahn so long that Brenner's perception of the infinite glide and soft ascent made him all the more certain of his prognosis: four-hour drive to Kitzbühel. Your sense of time gets a bit tricky in the dark, of course, and time in the trunk's always relative. Brenner was sticking to his prognosis now, although they hadn't been on the road more than two hours according to his sense of time. But his spaceship-trunk was also traveling at an incredible velocity.

Which Brenner ascertained from being stuck to the back wall the whole ride. He couldn't rule out the possibility that the milk and honey were still overpowering him for a few minutes longer.

And one thing you can't forget. When they exited the autobahn, he got chucked forward so brutally that it was like they were cruising at 250 into a well-cushioned wall. No chance to somehow absorb it, of course, when your hands are bound—in other words, nose and a rib. Because nose- and rib-wise Brenner took after his other grandfather, almost too delicate for his profession. Or then again, maybe not. It's exactly that kind of delicacy which you need. Brenner owed some important information about the speed they were traveling to his rib and nose—in other words, hellish. And without the rib, without the nose, it's possible that he would've thought it was too soon to be Kitzbühel. But he knew he could calmly cling to his assumption. Or, better put, he had to cling to it. Because you're not as apt to cling to a guess taken out of fear as you are to one taken out of, let's say, hope.

And this feels just like the road that runs through the town of Kitzbühel, he thought. His broken rib really didn't need that pothole before the right-hand turn. *And here we go steeply uphill, and those must be the switchbacks, and that's got to be Schotterstrasse now, and this here—where they're yanking me out of the trunk so savagely that I'm landing on the street with my broken rib and my broken nose and silencing the birds with my screams of pain, and where I'm polluting the majestic mountain air with my petrified sweat and where my teeth are biting into the sweet mountain grass—must be a place where there's no one near or far, i.e., in front of the cabin where I last saw Knoll alive.*

And this would have to be the door, if I'm not mistaken, being unlocked by that panting roughneck with the ghoulish nicotine fingers, that just muffled another scream of pain from my throat.

Look, sometimes you can guess as accurately as a clairvoyant and you can observe as closely as an Apache and the whole bit won't do you any good. Because if Brenner hadn't guessed so well, if he'd fooled himself, if he'd fallen prey to an illusion, or expected an apology for his unjust dismissal along the lines of, *Kressdorf is flying me to Las Vegas for a surprise concert*, and if Brenner was just now figuring out that he'd deceived himself—because in reality he'd just been shipped to Kressdorf's house in the mountains—then he wouldn't have been any worse off for it. In fact, he'd be in the same exact god-awful place. Because accurate predictions won't do you any good when you're locked in a trunk and can only predict that *soon I'll probably be in an even more hopeless place*. And even if you can predict with an almost uncanny clairvoyance that *after being freed from the trunk the nicotine fingers will hold a gun to my temple*, then you have no real advantage when it really does happen, except that you can be proud of what a good brain you've got waiting in your head for that gun.

But people are stubborn in this regard. Even in a hopeless situation, a person will still try to predict what's going to happen next. Because there's nothing else to be done. And Brenner, of course, was feverishly doing just that while his life was at its greatest risk—or would you say while his death was at its greatest risk? You see, I don't know anymore, life at risk or death at risk. Anyway, Brenner was in the middle of it, ninety-five and a half hours after the South Tyrolean stole Helena from his car, i.e., half an hour before the start of the fifth day.

Where exactly they'd locked him up wasn't difficult to guess, even with his eyes blindfolded. Because you can't forget the smell of the rabbit pen. The animals weren't there, of course, Kressdorf only got them on special occasions from their foster family. But the smell—merciless. It was the one thing that even the girls complained about when Bank Director Reinhard kept them behind the glass panel for hours on end before granting them a personal appointment. Congressman Stachl hated this quirk of Reinhard's because then the girls would smell like the pen, of course, especially their long hair—dreadful. And in a weak moment he'd even spoken with Kressdorf about whether Reinhard just didn't notice, whether his olfactory nerves were just that bad due to old age, or whether he was just making a point.

You can't be ungrateful, though, because the nicotine fingers that groped his face and tore off his blindfold weren't that bad now compared to the smell in the pen. Interesting, though: Brenner felt blinder without the blindfold. Because of the mirrored glass separating the hunters' den from the animal pen. From the other side you could see into his zone perfectly, but from the inside you couldn't see who was behind the glass, you could only see yourself. Reinhard liked it that way, that he could see the girls but they couldn't see him.

When you feel blind, your sense of smell intensifies, of course. And even Mr. Nicorette's sense of smell might have been slowly returning to him in his withdrawal period. Because he told his freckled friend now that he badly needed to get out into the fresh air, he was suffocating in here.

But the foreman shook his head and pointed outside, where the sound of a car being parked could be heard. "There's no time for that now. Just hurry up with him, then you can get some fresh air," he said and then left the two of them there in the pen together. Nicorette looked offended and stuck his white plastic pipe back into his mouth. And it was this piddly little straw, of all things, that terrified Brenner. Because an interrogator's cigarette would have been the protocol. Offer a cigarette, blow smoke in the face, *ever see a match burn twice*, and so on, all common cruelties, but the withdrawal pipe gave the thug a human quality, and a human quality is always life threatening.

"Did you know that decades of smoking reduces sperm count?" Brenner said. Because he thought he absolutely had to cover up how weak he was feeling.

The security guard from the construction site replied in his own way, i.e., with an attempt at ruining Brenner's sperm count for good. But the poor watchdog didn't have that much air left in him, because the kick sent sweat running down his forehead—you'd have thought it hurt him more than Brenner—and it was only after sucking on his straw a few more times that he'd pumped himself back up. He used his gangster patter on Brenner, he could find out fast or slow, nice or rough, however he liked—but anyway, what he was interested in: "Where's Helene?"

It looked a little strange, the construction-site guard, muscular as an ox, not a hair on his head but twenty-five tattoos on his thick neck to compensate, and he was sucking on the nicotine pipe like an infant. You can only say this in retrospect, but there's something tragic about someone still struggling to quit smoking even in the last hours of his life.

"What's that, Herr Simon? Cat got your tongue? Where've you got Helene?"

It struck Brenner that he pronounced her name about as wrong as the South Tyrolean and her Marl*boo*ro. And believe it or not, that reminded him of the only book that his grandparents had owned, or better yet, of a story in the four-inch thick *Pious Helene* by Wilhelm Busch. That's how the tattooed ox pronounced her name, like Pious Helene. No, that's not true, his grandparents had two books, the Wilhelm Busch and *The Doctor Pays a House Call.* And very good pictures in both! But around a certain age he stumbled upon *The Doctor*'s hiding place, and *Pious Helene* became boring to him, so from that point on, only *The Doctor*, don't even ask.

Brenner criticized the tattooed ox now, but not for pronouncing "Helena" like Pious Helene. He acted like it didn't bother him, because whoever has the gun gets to decide on matters of taste, that's true the world over. Instead, Brenner answered, "You know for a fact I'm the first person who'd like to know where the girl is."

"You're the first person who'd like to know? Before her parents, even, or what? Are you the one suffering here or what?"

"No. The first aside from her parents, of course."

Yup, you see here, the construction-site ox was just too stupid, because otherwise maybe he would've been able to detect from his hasty correction that Brenner was lying. But fine, analysis wasn't his job anyway. He was just in charge of the questions. For the analysis, that's what the gentlemen behind the glass were for. Don't forget the baby monitor that Kressdorf would sometimes switch on, much to Bank Director Reinhard's delight. He always liked listening to the girls babbling over it, background music, as it were, while he and Congressman Stachl negotiated life's serious matters. Brenner, of course, was thinking only of the gentlemen behind the screen now, as the tattooed ox sucked the next question out of his little straw. "If you don't want to say where Helene is—"

"Helena,"—now Brenner did interrupt him—"her name is Helena, and I don't know where she is."

"—then maybe you'd like to tell us where your friend Knoll is."

Ah, of course. Knoll. For the first time Brenner saw that he might have a chance to walk away from all of this with his life. He wasn't going to tell them where Helena was, in order to protect the South Tyrolean. He hadn't given any thought yet to his own survival. But now all of a sudden he saw a chance for Knoll to save him again.

He was focused so intently on the room behind the glass that it almost seemed like he could see how the Bank Director and the Construction Lion and the Congressman were sitting and observing him. But not just him; they must have been observing each other, too. He realized now that at least one of them didn't know anything about Knoll in the cesspit, or else they wouldn't be letting the ox ask such stupid questions.

"Why should I know where Knoll is?"

"Because maybe you were the last person he was seen with. Nothing goes unnoticed in a Schrebergarten, you should really know better."

"I followed Knoll there because I thought he would lead me to Helena."

After half a ton of ersatz nicotine, the tattooed ox found his tongue again. "And him acquiring Neighbor's Rights by purchasing that Schrebergarten dump, you didn't know anything about that either of course. And that his lawyer's already obtained a halt to the construction."

"I don't believe this!"

"What don't you believe?"

"That you care more about your fucking construction site than you do about the girl!"

The giant infant had nothing to say to that, but curiously sucked a new question out of his white plastic teat. "So why are you running after Sunny, if you have nothing to do with the video?"

"So why did you go and kill Milan because of it?"

Brenner thought this might be an interesting bit of news for one or another of the fine gentlemen on the other side of the glass, too. And truly the watchdog couldn't bring himself to answer it. The foreman stormed in, his mouth contracted so bitterly that it was smaller than his largest freckle.

"That was an occupational accident. Self-defense!" the talking freckle said. "The idiot pulled his toy gun. It's insane that those exact replicas aren't illegal!"

"Maybe it's the real ones that should be kept out of *your* hands and the kids should be allowed to have their fun."

"Well, it's your fault you picked such an amateur for this kind of business. But we won't hold it against you. Give us the video, and you can go home."

"I have several videos," Brenner said. "But no VCR. I

don't want to throw them away, either. They're still memories, even if I can't play them anymore."

"You know damn well we're not talking about a VHS cassette!" the tattooed ox shouted.

"A movie with Julia Roberts. A woman left it at my place when she moved back in with her husband."

The foreman whispered something into his security boss's ear, but Brenner simply kept talking.

"And then I've got another one with the 1976 men's Olympic downhill event on it, because I got stationed in Innsbruck when I was a young cop. At one point I'm even in the picture briefly with the queen of Sweden—back then she was just a hostess with the Olympic Committee, but now she's the queen of Sweden. That one I'm not erasing, of course. And at the end of the tape there's a Western. But the end got cut off."

Ninety-six hours after Helena's disappearance, the light went on over in the hunters' den, and Brenner saw who was behind the glass. It's always a bad sign for the victim, of course, when the perpetrator takes off his mask. Because by that point, no further police contact is expected. Interesting, though: for some reason, what unsettled him most was the fact that Bank Director Reinhard wasn't there.

CHAPTER 19

Ninety-six hours after Brenner had deliberated too long over which chocolate bar he should buy, Kressdorf and Congressman Stachl were standing to the left and the right of the open cesspit like two altar boys at a funeral. They looked up at the wooden balcony, where the two workers were slowly lowering Brenner down, direction: cesspit.

"Stop!" Kressdorf called out, when Brenner's feet were still just barely in the dry. He was so businesslike that you'd have thought he was helping the crane operator at the construction site set down a slab of concrete. Then, he amicably invited the dangling chauffeur once more to tell them where the video was that Knoll had given him. Nothing better occurred to Brenner than to curse Knoll loudly for having lied about leaving the video with him. It didn't do him any good, of course. He'd gotten the photo of Sunny from Knoll, so they weren't apt to believe that he had no clue what kind of video they were talking about. There were a thousand possibilities, from child pornography to—. There's nothing that doesn't exist in the world. I'd even say that the biggest mistake in our world is that there aren't at least a few things that don't exist. Because more often than not, non-things and non-people are far more likable than those who've pushed themselves elbows first into the world. Or have a look for yourself: non-ideas! Then non-opinions, non-feelings, non-loves, non-conversations, non-thoughts! I'll say it up front to all of them, *walk right in, my door is wide open for you!*

It's always difficult with existences. That's where the problems start. And they stop with the people who'll drag another person through the shit. Because of a video! And Brenner with no idea what's even on the video. But before you go conjuring thoughts into existence now, too, along the lines of *maybe Reinhard with the goat or Congressman Stachl with the rabbit*, I can tell you right now—all wrong. Completely off the mark. But Brenner didn't guess what was on the video, either.

"Lower!" Kressdorf called to the balcony. Stachl didn't say anything, he just glared at Brenner as though he was very mad at him for dragging him into this. And Brenner stared back at him as though he couldn't feel the gravy starting to seep into his shoes.

Still nothing of Bank Director Reinhard to be seen. A man like Reinhard wasn't going to be coaxed out of his domicile or his refuge for a minor incident. He didn't want to be bothered with the details. So he said, *Kressdorf and Stachl will take care of it*. And one thing you can't forget: delegating was an imposition to the good boss. Maybe he even would've liked to personally dunk each and every deserving person in the shit himself, but he had to leave it to his coworkers in order to motivate them. And the lower rung has to delegate it to the next rung below him, and so, when you're a Kressdorf or a Stachl, you can't dunk Brenner with your own hands when your musclemen have been waiting for months to have a little fun.

Efficiency was the only thing that was important to the bank director. And to that end, he'd chosen superb people. You've even got to hand it to them, for a hundred-million-euro project, two deaths aren't that many. Or three deaths, let's say, if you count the nanny's husband. And with his death, they didn't really accomplish anything; you'd be better off blaming the South Tyrolean. Strictly speaking, Knoll himself was guilty. And Milan, too, for being so extremely eager. But even if you were to tally them all up, you'd still have to say there are so many more deaths in the world that, for a hundred million euros, purely mathematically speaking, it still errs on the humane side.

Or four deaths, if you were to say that Brenner was headed that way, too, now. By this point, with the shit already tickling his kneecaps, Brenner himself wasn't placing any large bets on his life. And me neither, to be honest. Because he really didn't have any clue that Knoll's video surveillance system had happened to catch something completely different than what Knoll had been looking for. About that, I always say, most of the time people find something different than what they're looking for. So what did Knoll find on his surveillance videos? Pay attention, I'm only going to say so much. He couldn't have brought down the clinic with it. But it would've been enough for all of MegaLand.

In hindsight it would all be revealed eventually, or frankly, not even all of it, or else Vienna would look very different today, don't ask. But one thing you can't forget: Brenner's not in hindsight at this point. Not yet! Because it's just human nature that you're never in hindsight until it's too late. Although it's true, he was already in the gnats' realm, he'd been greeted warmly by them, he could even hover in the air a little, nonetheless he himself was no gnat yet. Whereas you might say, as a gnat maybe he would've been able to squint with his insect eyes from the other side of the globe, and with foresight, spot the very things which as a human you can only come to know with hindsight.

But no dice. Brenner knew nothing of the surveillance video. Well, if it had been a gas station surveillance video, he would've known everything; he would have been able to recite it backward and forward by heart, but clinic surveillance videos he knew nothing about, because that was Knoll's secret matter. And if you don't know something, you can't give it away, either. You can hang in shit up to your knees, it won't do any good. It might look like courage, but it's just stupidity. And as he sank even deeper, he looked like a Jesus with both legs amputated, crossing a shit sea on his stumps, but he still couldn't tell them where Knoll's surveillance video was because he didn't know and—cut.

Now what do you do in a situation like this, when you don't know anything, but your fellow man is torturing you in order to make you know something? A person's always got to do something; not doing anything isn't an option for us.

Most people scream their heads off at times like these, but Brenner didn't scream once, not even when the slurry reached his most ticklish spot. If you think about it in terms of getting into a swimming pool, then you know that the slurry had already risen above the hem of his swim trunks now, and you should know, when it came to the hem of his swim trunks, he took after his sensitive grandfather again.

And the rope let out even farther. Brenner didn't feel

any ground beneath his feet. He prepared himself for the eventuality that he'd soon feel Knoll with the tips of his toes and shortly thereafter he'd be lying down there beside Knoll, but he still didn't know what he was supposed to tell the criminals up above to make them pull him back out, and early enough that the lasting damages would be only psychological—sleepless nights, fear of every earthworm—but not bodily.

When I said that the hem of your swim trunks was uncomfortable, that applied to ice-cold swimming pools. For cesspools: the neck's much more uncomfortable. And Brenner would have been prepared to betray everything and everyone just so that they'd pull him back out. But the only pulling that the pigs were doing now was on the second rope that bound his legs—so that he couldn't stand on the tips of his toes anymore and keep his head above the slurry. His mouth would be free for a few more seconds, but he simply knew nothing about a video.

When he'd been completely under for a full minute or two, as he was starting to share the brotherhood of the cesspit with Knoll, it occurred to him, probably from the deoxygenation, what he had to tell them so that they would pull him out. He'd tell them that Helena would die if they killed him. That he'd hidden her in a basement, and if they killed him, the child would be left miserably alone to die of starvation.

Brenner, however, was already a little more into the next world than here in this world, of course. He was already so close to feeling eternal peace that he was mixing up the most important details. You should know, total peace is related on many levels to stupidity. Brenner's lack of oxygen was now to blame for his confusion over the before and after. In reality, of course, he'd said immediately that Helena would die a miserable death without him. It had occurred to him right away, instantly, the very first thing. Because normally when your life is in danger, your only trump hits you pretty fast. And when your death is in danger, you play it right away.

And Brenner was absolutely normal in this respect, too. In other words: instantly! He hadn't even been knee-deep in the cesspit when he howled: *Kid! Basement! Helena! Helene!* Because you can't forget that his life was in danger. That his death was in danger. And as his thighs were sinking, it had long ceased to be news to the two altar boys by the cesspit and the two gravediggers on the balcony, because he'd already howled it out the moment the shit started seeping into his shoes. Not just once, but ten times, a hundred times, *I have the kid*, so loud that somebody must have heard it down in Kitzbühel. I still say, someone should really investigate whether someone or other down in the village below heard Brenner—screaming for help, his life in danger—and didn't lift a finger because that's how people are!

Interesting, though: it didn't seem to him like he was sinking. More like the threat of death was sloshing up out of the earth to meet him. Like the threat to his life was inexorably rising, like sewer water, above his ankles, above his calves, above his knees, and not as if he were sinking ever deeper into the threat of death. Because our senses deceive us like crazy, especially considering the fumes. And even though he bellowed that he knew where Helena was and that she would die without him, it now seemed like he hadn't said anything, because it only occurred to him once it was too late.

If there is such a thing! But I say it's lucky that in such desperate situations, the human mind is prone to mercy. Just like how we often glorify things with age, and *it wasn't all that bad, when I was in the war I got to see Scandinavia, when I was in love I got to visit IKEA several times*, just as the consoling brain sometimes arranges the world in such a way that lets us think we had an impact. And when someone has cancer, then we say, *well, he could have prevented it, if he'd lived accordingly, because sunburn, alcohol, white flour, dark meat, dreary thoughts, and, and, and.* Or canoodling with a smoker twenty-eight years ago, i.e., nobody but yourself to blame for tongue cancer. And with self-blame, everything's instantly half as bad, because at least an impact was made. And so, with his senses dwindling, Brenner felt around for Knoll in the absolute darkness of the cesspit, and still managed to think: *I only have myself to blame because I should have said that I have Helena.* And so you see that in dying he was already entering the euphoric phase—and all because of self-blame—and that is the greatest fortune that you can have at the end of a fulfilled life.

Brenner was happy to meet someone he knew on the bottom of the cesspit, too. But not what you're thinking, Knoll. Because after sixty seconds in a cesspit—you get what I mean? By that point a person's generally resembling a gnat already, more soft wing tissue than legs and arms—eternal circulation more than crude perfection.

Now, who was it, if it wasn't Knoll? Watch closely: believe it or not, there on the bottom of the cesspit Brenner met the good lord. Of course it was a surprise, don't even ask. Well, for Brenner a surprise, not for the good lord, of course. He smiled benevolently from the other side of the cesspit, which seemed about as far away to Brenner now as the other end of a swimming pool. But regardless, no doubt who the man was. The very fact that he glowed. Iridescent understatement! You can't even imagine what a *Hello* that was for Brenner. Because first of all, he never really expected to meet the good lord even once—and if he did, then he expected a nice setting, with trumpets, with fanfare, with candlelight, with menus, with virgins, and, and, and. *But no*, Brenner thought—and he had to do a double take, he was so surprised to meet him in this unseemly place—*in a cesspit, covered in seven feet of shit, I meet the good lord.*

Interesting, though: the surprise visit didn't make Brenner nervous. Not even as the good lord came closer now. And one thing you can't forget: he moved insanely fast, he traveled faster than a light in the dark. And the closer he came, the better Brenner felt. Because the good lord, of course—charisma, don't even ask. To him, the lackluster surroundings didn't matter one bit. You hear that again and again, the real celebrities are uncomplicated. Prime example right now: the good lord. He just smiled when Brenner said, "So you do exist!"

To be perfectly honest, a slight note of indignance accompanied the surprise in Brenner's voice. "If I had known in my youth," he said to the good lord, "I would've had the girls lined up!" But then it didn't seem that important for him to complete the sentence anymore, and he thought to himself, *forget about it, main thing, don't let the opportunity go to waste. Just a pity that I can't tell anyone else now what a good guy he is!*

But "pity" and "reproach" and "main thing," the whole "alas" and "thank god," didn't mean anything real to Brenner anymore. You should know, when you're sitting in the good lord's lap, the earthly matters slip right past you. The Mega-Land stooges up above were already irrelevant to him, he wasn't even mad at them because—great terms with the good lord.

He only got angry when they pulled him out at the last second. And when his mind started up again, its explanations immediately kicked in, too, i.e., the light that Brenner had seen was only the light of day that he'd been heaved back into. His feeling of happiness was only triggered by the pleasant sensation of being lifted up and out of the cesspit. And the good lord's swift approach must have been triggered by his encounter with Congressman Stachl, who—just as Brenner was being brought back into the light—flew past him into the cesspit.

CHAPTER 20

It happens that fast in life. Congressman Stachl had just been standing up there among the people who were trying at all costs to find out where Brenner was keeping the video, and now he was the one lying in the cesspit and Brenner was back up above. Fortunately, Brenner's promise of information about Helena's whereabouts proved to be of greater interest to Kressdorf than the million-euro project after all, because—paternal instincts.

And when Congressman Stachl refused to haul Brenner back out, Kressdorf got his hunting rifle from the house and struck the congressman so forcefully on the back of the head that they later determined from the autopsy that Stachl hadn't drowned in the cesspit at all, but arrived there with his neck already broken. And so you see once again how much truth there is in the saying *practice makes perfect*. Say what you will about it. Because with Knoll they determined that Kressdorf had only knocked him out with the hunting rifle and it was in the cesspit that he died.

But don't go thinking that the two musclemen blindly listened to Kressdorf and pulled Brenner back out again. The opposite. It got to be much too much for them once Kressdorf completely lost it and went for the congressman.

They realized right away, of course, that they couldn't rely on Kressdorf anymore. And not on their stake in MegaLand either, since he was putting the project at risk. Watch closely. With a shotgun pointed at them, he had to force them to pull Brenner back out and untie him there beside the cesspit.

I've thought about it a lot since then, and I can thoroughly understand Kressdorf taking such drastic action, given that he'd learned just two days earlier that Helena wasn't his biological daughter. Now he saw his one and only chance to take back his fatherhood with force, by doing away with the sperm donor and rescuing Helena. And one thing you can't forget: after he'd clocked Knoll for rubbing it in his face that he wasn't even the father of his own daughter, it would've been pointless for Kressdorf to stop halfway.

Brenner, of course, wasn't waiting a moment's thought on these things now. He wasn't even aware at first that he was back up above. His senses hadn't completely returned to him yet when the shot rang out. And one thing you can't forget: a hunting rifle's always a loud shot. But that's not to say that Kressdorf was shooting into the air with his hunting rifle in order to return Brenner to his senses now—wake the dead, as it were. Quite the contrary. Kressdorf was helping his security boss—who didn't want to resuscitate Brenner—to quit smoking once and for all, i.e., shot him right in the lungs. And then the foreman did it gladly, though it was no pretty task, because let's put it this way: Brenner had more freckles on his face than the man who was respirating him. The foreman only did it because his boss was holding a shotgun to his head. But if you're saying, *that's despicable*, then I unfortunately have to tell you, this was still the nice part of the story.

And if you scare easily, think about something else now. Close your eyes and think of that vacation on the beach, reclining chair, suntan lotion, sound of the waves. And not of that patch of grass beside the cesspit. Kressdorf wasn't leaving anything half-done there. In other words, Brenner's first breath was also his rescuer's last. Because directly in the head. And believe it or not, Brenner almost envied him for it.

Normally you'd say that a person who's just come to should rest a little while and not return right away to the mob office that he's just taken a flying leap from until after a lunch break. But here again is the advantage of being the murderer. You don't have to go around agonizing about the little moral prescriptions. And Kressdorf wasn't going to begrudge Brenner the chance to catch his breath now. With shotgun in hand, he forced Brenner, who was still shaky and befuddled, to push the two corpses into the cesspit to join Knoll and Congressman Stachl. And you see, that's the beautiful thing about misfortune. That is the magnificent thing about sickness and death. That's the wonderful thing about exhaustion and collapse. You hopelessly outmatch every weapon. Because total exhaustion, terminal illness, complete despair, nothing's more motivating than a shotgun. But Brenner was just too exhausted still. Even with the strongest of wills, he couldn't do it. His knees kept buckling—marionettes haven't got anything on him.

There was nothing left for Kressdorf to do now. Shotgun or no shotgun, he had to do it himself. In the workplace, he'd heave a loud sigh at every opportunity and bemoan tearfully how he always had to do everything himself. But today, no whining, no sighing, and no stamping his feet. He was utterly focused on the matter at hand. I'd almost like to say it was one of the happiest moments in his life, when there was nothing except him and the task before him, and with a few determined kicks of his foot, he nudged the two corpses over the edge of the cesspit, where each disappeared with an indifferent splash.

My dear swan, Knoll, the congressman, and the two bully-boys in a cesspit. A party came together there, and you almost have to say, it's no minor feat when a pool of shit is made qualitatively worse.

Standing had become so strenuous for Brenner that he sat back down in the grass, right at the edge of the cesspit. He stared into it and tried to remember something important that he'd experienced down there. He mustered all his powers of concentration, but he only knew that it was something terribly important. Something earth-shattering, it seemed to him, that explained why he was so exhausted. But it sank deeper and deeper, never to resurface in him.

Purely from a detective's standpoint, it wasn't so bad that he'd completely forgotten the good lord because the good lord wasn't the perpetrator. The good lord didn't make the South Tyrolean take Helena. He didn't make Brenner forget to gas up the night before. He didn't make the Frau Doctor implicate her husband in a gigantic construction contract by not reporting an abortion she'd performed on a twelve-year-old child. He didn't make the congressman spoil Prater Park and get his contractor's wife pregnant. And above all, he didn't make Knoll make threats in his name.

The good lord just gazed upon all of this with a smile because—free will. The sight of the open pit, into which his memory had disappeared for all eternity, was so discomforting to Brenner that he asked Kressdorf whether he should cover the cesspit back up with the wooden boards or whether it wasn't worth it because he was still planning to throw him in, too.

"Close it up," Kressdorf said. "Why do you think I got you back out, Herr Simon?" Because—unbelievable, Kressdorf, still correct, addressing Brenner formally as Herr Simon. "You I still need. And those few boards can always be quickly removed again. But no innocent person should fall in."

Then he sent Brenner to the shower and had him put on some of his clean hunting clothes. And then they drove to Vienna to get Helena.

CHAPTER 21

One thing I've never liked about the human brain: that in the most dangerous situations, it often attaches importance to the silliest little things. So it bothers you that the executioner uses a bad aftershave, it bothers you that the doctor pronounces your throat cancer with a rolled *R*, and it bothers you that you can't claim your wedding ring as a tax deduction. And believe it or not, it was bothering Brenner now that he should have to slip into a hunting ensemble while Kressdorf nagged him.

But I have to defend Kressdorf here. What was he supposed to do? There simply wasn't any other clothing in the cabin. And was he supposed to let Brenner sit on his leather upholstery in his cesspit-soaked clothes? He didn't have to rush him, either, though. As if it were all riding on these few seconds now. Brenner only had two buckhorn buttons fastened when Kressdorf got impatient and pushed him into the car.

So that Kressdorf wouldn't notice how bad he was feeling, Brenner said in the car, "Today we're really contributing something to the rejuvenation of society." But Kressdorf didn't react, just kept his sights trained on Brenner so he wouldn't make a wrong turn on the way out of Kitzbühel. As if the joke-explaining soul of the newly deceased security guard were inside him, Brenner went on, "Because swapping four imbeciles for one child, society can't have anything against that."

But Kressdorf told him he should keep his mouth shut and concentrate on the driving. Whether or not he meant to address Brenner formally as Herr Simon was left open-ended this time because short and succinct: "Shut up."

As Brenner told him the story of the accidental kidnapping by the South Tyrolean, it seemed like he might actually be halfway reaching Kressdorf again, but no sooner had he begun to hope that his disclosure might turn Kressdorf around and pull him back over to his side, when Kressdorf interrupted him again with a perfectly devoid of emotion "Shut up."

At least this gave Brenner plenty of time to think about what his best course of action was in order to keep Kressdorf from shooting him as soon as he got the kid. Or if he did shoot him, how he could prevent him from shooting the South Tyrolean, too. Because one thing's clear: when you've come as far as Kressdorf has, you don't waste any time coddling your witnesses, no, you mop them up like fly droppings because—no sentimentality.

But the longer he thought about it, the more hopeless the situation seemed to him. Between Amstetten and St. Pölten, he tried to ensnare Kressdorf in conversation again. "What was it about your wife that Knoll caught on tape and you killed him for?"

"Nothing at all."

Interesting, though: because Brenner thought "Nothing at all" meant about as much as "Shut up," he didn't even entertain the possibility that Kressdorf had just begun to tell him the truth. But maybe Brenner's silence was good just now, because twenty kilometers outside St. Pölten, Kressdorf started talking again. "It wasn't my wife who Knoll found something out about. It was me. You know how my office is in Munich."

Kressdorf thought about this sentence for another five minutes, as if he'd discovered an explanation for all the world's misfortunes in the words "Munich" and "office."

"That's why I'd sometimes use my wife's office in Vienna and keep the bribe money in the clinic's safe. Once, Congressman Stachl met me there to deliver a kickback. And Knoll got it on his surveillance camera."

"How much was he demanding for it?" Brenner asked, because now that Kressdorf had gotten to talking, a question in between wasn't a problem anymore.

"Nothing at all. Knoll was an idealist. His suggestion was: he erases the tape, and I get my wife to close the clinic once and for all. If he'd gone public with his evidence, not only would MegaLand have been history, Congressman Stachl and I would've gone to prison, KREBA would've gone bankrupt. And so on. I'm not just talking about a few million euros."

That Kressdorf was telling him all this—ninety-nine hours after Helena's kidnapping—was not a good sign for Brenner.

"You know what I think?" Kressdorf asked him. But then he just thought it over for a while and kept it to himself. Whether he just wasn't certain, or he just didn't want to divulge it to Brenner, I don't know.

He said, "Knoll was always grinning with that air of superiority. Especially when I explained to him that I'd rather go to prison than cause my wife any harm. He just said, with that smug smile of his, that he didn't understand where Helena—"

Kressdorf sank so low now, it was as if he'd never speak another word again. Brenner almost finished the sentence for him, just to get it out there. He almost said, *this kind of thing has happened to other men before, too.* Almost said, *the main thing is that nothing's happened to Helena.* But Kressdorf didn't give the impression of wanting to hear anything more, so Brenner didn't say anything at all.

"What blood type are you, Herr Simon?"

"I don't know. They measured it once when I was on the force."

"Measured!" Kressdorf laughed. But it wasn't a laugh that eased Brenner's mind. Because it was the clipped, dry laugh of a ghost. "You mean tested."

"I don't remember, though."

"Why didn't you stay on the police force?"

Brenner didn't reply, because on the cue of "police," Kressdorf kept right on talking.

"I've done plenty of half-legal things in my life. Or illegal, as far as I'm concerned. Everybody knows that nothing happens in the construction business without bribes. And MegaLand is far and away the biggest contract KREBA's ever gotten. But real crimes, kidnapping and blackmail, I've never had anything to do with them. Not to mention murder. Or manslaughter. And when I pressured my wife to perform the abortion on that underage girl of Reinhard's, it was already too much for me. Not because of the abortion, but because of her. I told her that, what with the bank loan, Reinhard had Knoll right in the palm of his hand. That's why she did it. And to finally be left in peace by Knoll. But not even the bank director managed to subdue Knoll."

"Or he didn't want to," Brenner said.

"Or he didn't want to, exactly."

"But, all the same, you got into the MegaLand business because you smoothed the way with the abortion."

"That's correct, Herr Simon."

Brenner opted not to say anything more now, because he noticed that Kressdorf was in an overly sensitive mood where he was interpreting everything as a reproach.

"And then the congressman went into business with my wife." Kressdorf laughed so bitterly at that, you would've thought it was a worse crime than the four people dead in the cesspit.

"Stachl and I met at a charity golf game. I'd been after him for years. Like every other contractor. Before, he'd always brushed me off like I was just some do-it-yourself builder and he was Donald Trump. But then all of the sudden he was sweet as pie. He whispers to me that Bank Director Reinhard has a problem that my wife can remedy. And in turn, Reinhard might have an opportunity to subdue Knoll."

"And to let you build MegaLand."

"Don't be ridiculous. It's not that easy to build in Prater Park. It started with the golf course, and then it grew from there. For a banker who was in the black, it was a matter close to his heart for half of the Prater to come under his control, and right in the middle of Vienna when the whole city's in the red. With Stachl he had the right man at his side. People's protests did in fact hold us up, but we just about had them all cleared out of our way. Then suddenly Helena was kidnapped. We thought Knoll was behind it. And Knoll thought we were behind it. And now you're telling me it wasn't even an actual kidnapping. But in the meantime, four people are dead."

"Six," Brenner said, "if you count Milan and the nanny's husband."

"Stachl tried to keep me from pulling you back out. He said, 'Too much has happened already.' It didn't matter to him one bit that Helena was his kid, too."

"Maybe he didn't know?"

Kressdorf had nothing to say to that. I almost think it didn't matter to him either at this point.

When they arrived in front of the South Tyrolean's house, across the street from the gas station, Brenner still didn't know how he was supposed to keep the humiliated non-father from killing both him and the South Tyrolean in order to undo history and get his daughter back, not just Helena, but hair, skin, all of her—genetically speaking, as it were.

Now, for your reassurance. At least the South Tyrolean wasn't there.

Now, for your disassurance. The child wasn't there, either.

After they'd searched the last room, Brenner tried to convince Kressdorf that he hadn't lied to him. He explained to him that the South Tyrolean had probably gone to the police after he didn't come back as promised. Even Brenner didn't really believe that, although it later turned out to be true. But then Kressdorf did something that filled Brenner with such fright that being dangled from a balcony seemed like a MegaLand attraction by comparison.

You should know, Kressdorf's angry outbursts had caused him so much damage both professionally and personally over the years that at some point, as a matter of principle, he'd taken to the age-old trick of silently counting down from ten in hairy situations. But Kressdorf was so far outside himself now that—one hundred hours after his daughter's disappearance—he forgot about the "silently" part, and although he was indeed counting down, he was doing it out loud.

"Ten."

When a grown man just starts doing this, it's a little creepy maybe, but when he's already deposited four people in a cesspit, and when you can only hear him counting with your right ear because the barrel of his rifle is in your left ear, then you've got Brenner's situation exactly.

"Nine."

Kressdorf took a deep breath, exhaled deeply, inhaled deeply.

"Eight."

Brenner didn't breathe at all.

"Seven."

Now, while Kressdorf's slowly counting down so as not to make a mistake because of his temper, I'll tell you something else real quick now. Pay attention. How did they even get into the apartment? The South Tyrolean hadn't given Brenner a key. And Kressdorf's not one to break down a door. He's not that type of full-service criminal, who you might say, learned the trade from the bottom up, who can do everything from a bike lock to a clean kidney stitch. Kressdorf had only the brutality, the buttoned-up uncompromisingness that you learn in the Business School of Life, but craft and skill, zero. He stood before that locked door like a cow before a gate.

Brenner, on the other hand. He could have forced him, i.e., gun to the head, to break down the door. First of all, though, Brenner had never been particularly good at breaking down doors, he'd gotten a D in breaking down doors at the police academy. And above all, why should Brenner break down the door when he'd seen where the South Tyrolean hides her keys a few times now? Because she said she'd locked herself out with the damn spring lock three times already, and burglars are going to find a way in anyway, so she might as well leave a key for herself, too. Whether you believe it or not, in a *ficus benjamina*.

"Four."

You'll have to excuse me for going into such detail, but it just never fails to amaze me how between a perfectly normal *ficus benjamina*, between perfectly normally unlocking the door, between a perfectly normal look in the bedroom, look in the kitchen, look in the bathroom, look in the twenty-five rooms filled with plants, look in the closet, between the perfectly normal disappointment of not finding what you're looking for, and a disappointed perp shooting you in the head—often a matter of just a few seconds.

"Three."

And the earth turns quietly on. Purely from the universe's point of view, it makes no difference whether Kressdorf squeezed the trigger or not—as far as I'm concerned, it's no greater difference than whether the key's hidden in a ficus tree or a rubber plant. No greater difference than the question, *was the key made by Mr. Minute or Key Central?* To the universe all of it means absolutely nothing, and does Brenner or does he not have a hole in his head, will he die now or in twenty years, will he die quickly or slowly, will he die in despair or at peace with himself and the world, will he die excruciatingly or painlessly—to the universe it's all the same, you can't even imagine. Was Brenner even born or was he aborted in maybe the third or fifth month—either way it's the same to the universe—as if his mother were in her six-hundred and eighty-ninth month, but still no cash on delivery.

"Two."

Brenner was on the exact same page as the universe now. He didn't care whether Kressdorf pulled the trigger or not, either. And from that you can tell just how afraid he really was. How convinced he was that Kressdorf would snuff him out in an instant. How far into the hereafter he was already projecting himself. How he was basically looking forward to flying with the gnats—because he didn't remember the good lord anymore, but flying's a classic human dream.

"One."

Interesting, though—Kressdorf lowered the gun barrel now and pointed it at Brenner's heart. But the blood, oh the blood, my god all the blood—one hundred hours after the girl's disappearance—ran down Brenner's forehead and through his hair and across his cheeks and over his whole face.

The world just about flipped on its head, like with Herr Jesus, how you always see him hanging naked on the cross, because they nailed him to it so he wouldn't fall down, but then on top of that, he's got this wound in his emaciated ribcage because he hadn't been able to nab much at the last supper. And so that always means the soldiers had to stick him in the heart to hedge their bets, because you never know exactly when it's just the cross—maybe he's just playing dead, and then will walk away from it. The pierced heart is on every Jesus's right, though, which is the wrong side. I think they stuck it in below the ribs and then up heartward, well thought out by the soldiers. But why was Brenner's blood shooting an undammed river over his face when the shotgun had been pointed at his heart?

Simple explanation. It wasn't Brenner's blood. It was Kressdorf's blood. After one hundred hours, in the middle of the fifth day, Kressdorf's head burst into pieces, because a bullet from Detective Peinhaupt's gun had hit him so precisely that it probably would've wrecked the whole splendid old room—the philodendron and the rubber plant and the cyclamen and the asparagus fern and the avocado and the Busy Lizzie and the orchids and the bamboo and the ivy and the Christmas cactus and the azalea all would have been full of blood—if Brenner hadn't absorbed most of it, that is.

Maybe that doesn't sound so pretty, but in all honesty, Brenner hadn't felt this good in a long time. In spite of having missed his last two pills. But, old saying, nothing helps a depressive mood more than a bullet that misses you by a hair.

CHAPTER 22

The first body to be released for burial was the nanny's husband, probably because when you're the police, there's no lack of certainty over a death that you pulled the trigger on. There weren't many people there, but Brenner gave the Frau Doctor, of all people, credit for coming to the funeral, even though the man had tried to profit from her misfortune. And whether you believe it or not, she even let the nanny continue to look after Helena. On the one hand, as a single parent you're happy to have anyone at all for your child, but I can imagine that the Frau Doctor was looking to blame herself once again, along the lines of, *if my child hadn't been in her care, then her husband never would've had the opportunity—and maybe, without me, they would've grown old together as a happily married couple.*

As they lowered his coffin into the cremation furnace, it struck Brenner that the Frau Doctor was crying more than the nanny, but surely her own losses played a role here—because she was really a double widow what with Kressdorf and Congressman Stachl—and it all might have flowed into her tears for the thirty-year-old dilettante sidecar driver, who they lowered to the sound of a cassette recording of his favorite song, "Above the Clouds," because his dream job: pilot.

Two days after Herr Zauner they buried Milan. Zauner, that was the nanny's husband's name, not Resch like the nanny because they were only life partners. You see, you get to know people at a funeral. Milan's name was Milan Zeco, and three days before his twenty-second birthday he got nailed. At first Brenner was surprised that the authorities would release a stabbing victim so soon based on his witness testimony alone. But then at Kressdorf's funeral, Peinhaupt told him that Sanja had corroborated his testimony. Which is to say, Milan had put himself between the two thugs so that Sanja could run away. But unfortunately he'd pulled his toy gun, and that was the mistake. Don't go thinking that Sanja was at the funeral, though. Either she didn't dare to go, or else Reinhard had told her she wasn't allowed to, I don't know.

The two gas station drunks were there. And they cried for Milan—Brenner hadn't seen anything like it his whole life. Preimesberger, Erich, so the fat one was named, born 1967, sign Pisces, Capricorn ascendant, and the thin one was Strobl, Peter, December '65, Sagittarius, ascendant unknown.

Brenner learned all of this at a Shell gas station by the cemetery where they drank to Milan. They deliberately drove past a BP station that was closer by, i.e., one-day funeral boycott since the BP company had fired Milan over nothing.

Brenner's cell phone didn't ring once the whole time they were at the gas station, but Preimesberger, Erich must have had an incredibly good sense of hearing, because after a few beers he started humming, pitch perfect, "Castles made of sand fall in the sea eventually." Just for fun, to pull Brenner's leg. And believe it or not, it wasn't until that moment when

Brenner heard it as just a hummed melody that the missing lyrics finally hit him, as though Jimi Hendrix had tried to warn him from the start that MegaLand would cause him mega-problems. And, I should add, he really would've needed to tune in better to hear what Jimi Hendrix had been telling him. Or, for those who don't believe in Jimi Hendrix, the unconscious mind. Because why else would Brenner have picked out this song, which had never been his absolute favorite, just a few weeks after he took the job? You see, so it begins.

Annoyed that this was only just clicking into place for him now, he switched his ringtone back to normal right there in the Shell shop. Or, better put, he couldn't do it himself, but Strobl, Peter—incredibly adept at this sort of thing.

Three beers later he wouldn't have been able to do it anymore, because he'd need both hands to hold onto the counter. Brenner paid for everything, out of sheer gratitude that they were content to blame Milan's death on BP and not on him. At least three of the fifties from the envelope Reinhard had given Brenner were put to practical use here.

In retrospect, the seven funerals seemed like one single long funeral to Brenner, even though nearly three weeks passed between the first and the last. It's always fascinating when human paths cross, and two people can be born a thousand kilometers apart, grow up on different continents, never hear of each other, and then by some fatal accident while on vacation they should meet. And it was exactly the opposite for the four in the cesspit now. They would've been buried together, but first they had to be fished out, and of course autopsies had to be performed, and so they landed in four different cemeteries.

For the security boss, Brenner even had to drive all the way to the Czech border, because he was interred in Gmünd. Nobody recognized Brenner in Gmünd because, even though he'd been in the newspaper again, this time as a liberated Kressdorf-hostage, black bars had been put over his eyes. At first the funeral seemed a little strange to him, but then he realized that the parents of the deceased were Jehovah's Witnesses, ergo their own rites and rituals. And after the funeral he had to call the ÖAMTC because the Mondeo wouldn't start. But don't go thinking that the Jehovah's Witnesses in Gmünd had something against him. Because a marten had chewed through the fuel line.

For the foreman, he also had to drive outside of Vienna, but only half an hour out to Tulln. You should know, Vienna's workers generally come from the surrounding areas—Waldviertel: the forest region, Weinviertel: the wine region, Bucklige Welt: land of a thousand hills, Burgenland: the sunny side of Austria, Steiermark: Austria's green heart—never from Vienna itself. Because the Viennese, generally speaking: lazy hogs. The foreman had a twin brother who resembled him down to the last freckle. And that was enough to make your skin crawl. Like the deceased was standing at his own grave site! The brother was a very decent male nurse at a regional hospital in Krems. The little girl at his side really looked like Pippi Longstocking what with her pigtails, and Brenner wondered whether she was the daughter of the dead or the living twin.

Interesting, though: regardless of whether it was her

father or her uncle lying in the coffin, Brenner had enormous sympathy for this girl, who he didn't know and hadn't known about. But a few days later at Kressdorf's funeral, when he saw Helena again for the first time—zero feelings. If that's even possible! He cast an aloof glance at her from across the church pews to where she stood holding her mother's hand behind the coffin. As though he hadn't spent days fearing for her life. As though he hadn't been holding on to a chocolate bar for weeks just for her. And he even forgot to give it to her now. I can't fully explain it, but maybe a psychologist could, who might say, *such and such, and therefore, Brenner, at that moment, no feelings.*

And while I'm on the topic of psychologists: maybe that's where the answer lies, and Brenner paid no attention to Helena because he was so worked up about Natalie. Or, actually about Peinhaupt, because he wondered what the cop was doing hanging around Natalie this whole time. What was there for him to go snooping around for at a funeral?

Brenner was of two minds. Because on the one hand, you shouldn't be ungrateful to the person who saved your life; on the other hand, Peinhaupt had interrogated him so much the last few days that he could have gladly done without him. And one thing you can't forget: as a cop, you don't usually go to the funeral of a criminal who you shot dead.

At least Peinhaupt didn't go to the congressman's funeral. Neither did Natalie. And even with the best of intentions, the Frau Doctor couldn't go. The newspaper people would have pounced on her, don't even ask. You should know, Stachl's murder by Kressdorf was hyped as the jealousy drama of the year—*Othello*'s got nothing on it. They couldn't get enough of the "double widow" who got her child back on the same day that she lost both of her men.

They didn't know anything about the bribes, because that was the small deal that the cops and the politicos and Brenner and Bank Director Reinhard all agreed on: that a connection didn't need to be established unnecessarily between the jealousy drama and MegaLand. And for that they were willing to cooperate with Brenner on the matter of the South Tyrolean, i.e., the South Tyrolean was released and was only charged for having waited as long as she did before turning the stray child in to the police.

You're going to say, Brenner could've quietly exposed the construction mafia so that even the big guys would get theirs, too. But what good would that have done? Stachl and Kressdorf were dead, and everything that would eventually come to light would get blamed on the two of them. And so Brenner just said, *I'd rather see if I can set things right for the South Tyrolean. Because who's going to water her flowers if she's locked away for months?* And so you see, there was also some self-interest involved, because he was worried that she'd ask him to water the flowers.

When he called and informed her that she didn't have much to fear, all she said was, "I knew from the shtart that you were a decent man. But could you do me a favor?"

Brenner was a little disappointed, of course, because in his opinion he had just done her a favor. On the other hand, he was glad for the chance to see her again. You should know, to his question *what kind of favor?* she'd only say, "Not over the phone. But if you're here in twenty minutes, the eshpresso will shtill be warm."

Her apartment felt a little strange to him at first.

"Everything's new in here."

And from Brenner's mouth, a sentence like that isn't a compliment.

"Because of the blood, I needed a painter and a floor sander. And because of the painter and the floor sander, I had to move the furniture outshide. And because they were already outshide, I let them get hauled away. I'm happy to be rid of that old junk."

"And the plants?"

"They're in the other rooms. I jusht have to put them back again."

"And that's what you couldn't say over the phone? That's what you dragged me here for?"

"The plants I can move by myshelf. But maybe only a few. It's gotten to be too many. I'm not some ape living in a jungle, you know."

"I liked them."

"I didn't realize you were such a greenhorn."

"So then, what do you need me for?"

Beaming, the South Tyrolean led him to the kitchen window and pointed to the street, where a factory-new VW bus with dealer plates was parked.

"You'll have to drive the car for me. I haven't driven in so long. It would be a pity if I drove it wrong."

"A VW bus?" A laugh nearly escaped Brenner. "What do you want a VW bus for?"

"So I can give somebody a ride now and then."

On the drive, she sat beside him beaming like a kid on her confirmation day and alternated between watching

Brenner and watching the pedestrians and the cars and the bicyclists and the shops. And every few minutes when Brenner pressed on the gas or the brakes or made a turn, expectantly she'd ask: "And? How's it drive?"

"Perfectly," Brenner replied, but meanwhile he started up on how a smaller, women's car would've been better for her, a Polo or a Mini or a French Musketeer or a Japanese Micra Mouse, and whether she couldn't still trade in the bus. But he might as well have been talking to the windshield, because at the next traffic light, the South Tyrolean, expectant again, asked, "And? How's it drive?"

"I need to step on it a little more," Brenner said, and he drove along the Danube in the direction of Klosterneuburg. Within a few meters of the road sign he was already going 120, and satisfied, the South Tyrolean determined, "It's got zing."

When the mighty bronze lions at the waterworks whisked past them, she beamed and said, "It's good to get away from your own shtreet now and then."

And believe it or not, it turned out that for the last three and a half years she hadn't dared to venture any farther from her apartment than the few meters to the gas station across the street. Until the day Brenner hadn't come back as promised and she'd set off to take Helena to the police.

Brenner didn't want to believe her at first, but she just said, "They've got everything at the gas shtation."

From her mouth, it sounded like a reasonable explanation for why she hadn't left her own street for three and a half years. Brenner was just glad she'd had the courage to on the day that she'd saved his life. So many unusual things had happened to him these past few days that he didn't try for very long to understand why a person would lock herself up at home for three and a half years. *"Confession" comes from "Comprehension,"* he thought, but he couldn't even comprehend why this nonsense would occur to him right now. And I've got to say, on closer examination, the normal person's a rarity, and should you ever meet him, you'd be better off asking him *how* and *why* and *how come.*

The VW bus ran perfectly in the mountains, too. Brenner drove it up to Reinhard's domicile, and incredibly, it was only on the steepest ten meters that he had to downshift to second.

It was early afternoon, and the bank director, of course, wasn't at his domicile. But his wife was lying in a lawn chair, her face in the shade, her legs in the sun. And you see, a bus is good for this, because Brenner wouldn't have been able to see over the bushes in a car that was any lower to the ground.

"Why did you park here?"

The South Tyrolean looked a little anxious, and to be perfectly honest, the steeply sloping street looked a little criminal. But the bus didn't roll away while Brenner walked briskly over to the garden gate and rang the bell. Reinhard's wife reluctantly got up from her lawn chair and came to the garden gate in a bathrobe. Brenner pressed an envelope into her hand and said he was supposed to deliver it to her husband. Three of the twenty fifties were missing, but Brenner didn't care.

On the drive back, he explained to the South Tyrolean why he'd returned the bank director's money, and because they were on the topic of money, he asked her what the VW bus cost.

"I bargained him down to fifty thousand," the South Tyrolean said, "radio included."

Because Brenner was still annoyed that she hadn't bought a more affordable women's car, he let the question slip, did she have a money tree?

"You might put it that way," the South Tyrolean replied, and she told Brenner that half of the valley back home belonged to her because her brother had a motorcycle accident and her uncle didn't have any children. "So I inherited my own megaland."

"And you sold off a field for the VW bus?"

"Are you crazy? I didn't give anything away. I shwore to myself that I wouldn't touch any of it. It's all leased out. And someday I'll leave it to someone else."

"And the fifty thousand?"

"That was last year's interesht on the savings account," the South Tyrolean said. "I thought the interesht I could at leasht touch for a car. So I can get out a little. It's not healthy to be cooped up on your own shtreet all the time. A person's got to be among people now and then."

It hit Brenner just then that he was due shortly at Knoll's funeral, and he asked her whether he could drive straight to the Döblinger cemetery, and she'd drive herself home.

"I don't undershtand why you go running to every single funeral," the South Tyrolean said. "You're worshe than my old aunties back home."

But Brenner didn't let that dissuade him, and because the South Tyrolean said nothing against it, he simply drove straight to the Döblinger cemetery and said good-bye to her.

But then he had to look. Because more people had come to Knoll's funeral than to Kressdorf's and Stachl's and Milan's and Herr Zauner's and the foreman's and the security boss's all put together.

Knoll was officially regarded as Kressdorf's first victim—not to mention a victim of slander, because of the public's rush to judgment about the kidnapping. In light of the murder, his smaller misdemeanors like blackmailing slipped right under the table—he was getting a hero's funeral now, you can't even imagine. From Opus Dei to the pope's best friend, from the last Habsburger to the cathedral preacher, they all came together to pay their last respects to the martyr. And right in the midst of the mourners Brenner discovered Bank Director Reinhard. He looked rather troubled. Because, I think for a benevolent string-puller like him it's always incomprehensible when your little ward—for whose mission he'd truly done what he could, even financing, without any collateral, the abortion clinic's surrounding offices—turns around and bites the hand that feeds him.

It came as no surprise to Brenner that he'd see Natalie at the funeral because over the years she'd sought out conversations with Knoll time and again. She told Brenner a few things about Knoll's life, that his father had been one of the first organic farmers and had died of skin cancer, and that the police still hadn't found the video.

"Maybe it doesn't even exist," Brenner said, and he wondered how Natalie got to be so well informed about the police investigation.

But when he saw who picked Natalie up after the funeral, everything became clear to him.

"Don't you have anything better to do than to go ogling after shtrange women?"

Brenner thought he wasn't hearing correctly. Knoll's funeral had lasted an hour and a half, and the VW bus was still parked there.

"How come you didn't drive home?"

"You're really not too shwift."

"It lasted too long for my taste, too."

"I'm talking about your head. It's not too shwift."

"That's what you said the first time we met at the gas station."

"And unfortunately it hasn't gotten any better."

Brenner stood in the parking spot and the South Tyrolean leaned out the open car door and spoke slowly, as though to a slow-witted child, "I don't have a driver's lischense, Herr Simon!"

And now that really reminded Brenner of the first time they met. Because just like then, he was searching for a good line, and just like then, nothing came to him. And so the South Tyrolean beat him to it.

"I'm going to need a chauffeur, Herr Simon."

"How do you figure that?"

"Firsht up, you drive me home."

That was a good suggestion for Brenner, because he was thinking, *by the time we get to her apartment, I'll have come up with a good excuse.*

As they drove out of the cemetery's parking lot they passed Natalie again, who was standing with Peinhaupt in front of his car and giving him a very serious talking-to. And Peinhaupt was looking rather grim, too. Desperate, I dare say.

Brenner would learn the reason why just thirty-seven weeks later. But just Peinhaupt's luck: Natalie was already well over forty, but she broke it to him after the funeral that, as of March, he'd be paying alimony for a fifth child.

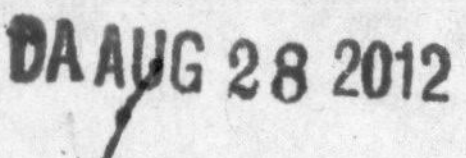

MELVILLE INTERNATIONAL CRIME

Kismet
Jakob Arjouni
978-1-935554-23-3

Happy Birthday, Turk!
Jakob Arjouni
978-1-935554-20-2

More Beer
Jakob Arjouni
978-1-935554-43-1

One Man, One Murder
Jakob Arjouni
978-1-935554-54-7

The Craigslist Murders
Brenda Cullerton
978-1-61219-019-8

Death and the Penguin
Andrey Kurkov
978-1-935554-55-4

Penguin Lost
Andrey Kurkov
978-1-935554-56-1

The Case of the General's Thumb
Andrey Kurkov
978-1-61219-060-0

Nairobi Heat
Mukoma Wa Ngugi
978-1-935554-64-6

Cut Throat Dog
Joshua Sobol
978-1-935554-21-9

Brenner and God
Wolf Haas
978-1-61219-113-3

Murder in Memoriam
Didier Daeninckx
978-1-61219-146-1

He Died with His Eyes Open
Derek Raymond
978-1-935554-57-8

The Devil's Home on Leave
Derek Raymond
978-1-935554-58-5

How the Dead Live
Derek Raymond
978-1-935554-59-2

I Was Dora Suarez
Derek Raymond
978-1-935554-60-8

Dead Man Upright
Derek Raymond
978-1-61219-062-4

The Angst-Ridden Executive
Manuel Vázquez Montalbán
978-1-61219-038-9

Murder in the Central Committee
Manuel Vázquez Montalbán
978-1-61219-036-5

The Buenos Aires Quintet
Manuel Vázquez Montalbán
978-1-61219-034-1

Off Side
Manuel Vázquez Montalbán
978-1-61219-115-7

Southern Seas
Manuel Vázquez Montalbán
978-1-61219-117-1

Death in Breslau
Marek Krajewski
978-1-61219-164-5